# These U[illegible]n

*A novel by E.J. Babb*

First published digitally in Great Britain 2018



Published under Bothersome Books

www.bothersomebooks.com



Cover design and imagery by Carl Doherty
Editing by Carl Doherty (www.shelfabuse.com)

*For Carl.*

*I shouldn't say this, but I write in a bid to impress you.*

*I hope it worked*

# 1

Most would waver by the door before announcing themselves, sidestepping apologetically into the room as if reluctantly intruding on a private moment. I hated all that. To me the room was empty, save myself and the patient.

The case was simple: Mrs Furstein was seventy-three years old and had been admitted to the facility with advanced dementia. The fact that her condition had been allowed to reach such a severe state could have been interpreted as negligence, but I suppose her family's judgement had been somewhat skewed by accountability.

The patient's husband was squeezed onto the bed beside her with his face nuzzled deep into her neck, yet his devotion was of little consequence; she was watching her loosely cupped hands because they were in close proximity to her face, not because she recognised the fingers attempting to intertwine with hers. She also failed to acknowledge her three adult children standing dutifully in the corner of the room, all looking to the floor so as not to make eye contact with the being that resembled their mother.

"What's going on." The husband spoke without question in his voice as I approached the bed, the white of his eyes reflecting the light as he tracked my every move.

I contemplated peeling him off of his murmuring wife so I could continue with my work, but instead looked to the fob watch attached to my right breast. “It is... three thirty-five exactly, Mr Furstein,” I said, “the treatment is scheduled for four o’clock.”

I didn’t wait for a response, which no doubt would have been one of contention. Taking an alcohol swab from the trolley I held and extended the patient’s rubbery forearm and smeared the solution onto her skin. With my left hand still gripping the wrist, I popped an empty syringe out of its plastic casing with my right and lined the needle up against a prominent vein.

“What are you doing?”

For the sake of civility I drew back slightly but kept the needle in line with its target. “Cataloguing her blood, Mr Furstein. It’s standard practice before treatment.” I knew he was aware of this as I had reminded him of the process mere hours before, but I felt duty bound to explain myself again.

While Mr Furstein was busy heaving himself into the sitting position, I quickly extracted a vial of blood from the patient, which was remarkably rich-looking despite the pale flesh that encased it. The wound was addressed before Mr Furstein had the chance to refocus.

I turned to hand the blood to the phys aid, whose gaze remained on the patient’s husband. “Should I take that to the lab,” she asked slowly, “or do you need me here?”

“Take it,” I said, thrusting the vial into her hand. She nodded reluctantly and left.

As I began readying for the procedure, Mr Furstein leaned across the bed to watch me, his hand mechanically stroking his wife’s hair as she whimpered. “Does she really need all this?” he asked, nodding to the trolley of equipment. “I’m starting to think this is all a mistake. I want to take her home, doctor.”

“Mr Furstein, I’m not a doct...” I stopped myself from clarifying my role to him once again. If it comforted him to think of me as a doctor then I would have to allow it. He clearly wasn’t capable of retaining any information about my profession. In any case, it wasn’t the first time I had had to repeatedly explain my role to someone and it certainly wouldn’t be the last. I’ve always found the public’s continued misconception of my work baffling. Familiarity, it seems, is far more comforting than progress.

Mrs Furstein’s mouth made an ‘o’ shape as I administered the muscle relaxant. She sank deeper into the bed, jaw slack and limbs limp, but Mr Furstein continued to paw at her. It was three forty-two and I was getting behind schedule.

“Mr Furstein, you’re going to have to move away from your wife for a moment.”

“No, please don’t make me leave her yet, I can’t.”

“You don’t have to leave her, just give her a bit of room. I think you’re hurting her.” I picked up her wrist to show the swollen finger marks he had left.

The old man dithered between getting up and lying back down. As he began to weep, all I could think was how much simpler it would be if medical opinion were enough, if it were the stronger argument against the cruel, selfish motives of the family, but society deems sentiment capable of overruling logic. DNA has always trumped education and experience.

It was three forty-four. I looked to his children for assistance but their blank faces reflected their father’s fears. Like him they were unable to appreciate the critical nature of the procedure, their silence forming a reluctant alliance with him.

I knew what they all needed me to say, I just had to get the words out convincingly.

I took a breath. “Trust me,” I finally managed, pushing the old man’s arm as gently as I could away from the patient, “this is the best thing you could be doing for her.”

As predicted, all he had needed was the permission to let go. He instantly moved away and perched on the edge of the bed, although a protective arm still rested on her shoulder.

Checking Mrs Furstein’s vitals took just a few minutes. She watched me calmly as I worked, holding herself as still as possible as if she knew I was trying to help her. She had been an easy patient to soothe throughout her stay at the facility, permitting anyone to dress, feed or examine her with no reaction other than a slow blink.

It was rarely the patients that complicated matters.

The final stage before the procedure was the preparation of the forms. On the table at the foot of the bed I set up five eGreement pads side by side, each with differing legal statements outlining the treatment and the potential risks involved. The forms were nothing more than a formality as the pre-procedural documentation was iron clad, but as medical proxy Mr Furstein was still required to demonstrate his acceptance of the treatment before anything could go ahead. Regulations have eased considerably over the years since the Furstein case, but there is still a lingering need for the profession to cover itself with endless witnessed signatures.

Once the pads were ready I offered the stylus to Mr Furstein. "If I could just ask you to sign these, sir, I need a signature on each before we can get started."

It was three forty-seven.

"I can't do this," he mumbled, his voice barely audible. "I can't sign them, I just don't think she needs this yet. I could take her home and look after her again."

I couldn't disguise my frustration as I exhaled heavily through my nose. "I'm afraid that's not possible. Either you sign these now and we go through with the procedure today or we'll be forced to obtain a court injunction against you, which could take weeks. I'm sure that would cause a lot of stress for you and your wife will be very poorly by then. We've been working towards this for a while now, haven't we? You know how ill she is. All you have to..."

Mr Furstein leapt forward, knocked the stylus out of my hand and grappled for the forms. I spread my arms out to protect the pads but his two sons had already grabbed him by the shoulders and had hauled him onto the nearest chair. Mr Furstein rasped and wheezed having winded himself in the struggle.

"Mr Furstein, please try and remain calm," I said, although my words would have made little impact if they had been heard. I sounded hollow and weary even to myself.

Mr Furstein gave a dry cough. "You can't take her now, not yet. Something will go wrong, I know it, and I wouldn't be able to live with myself. She's all that's ever mattered to me. I can't let you do this... *please*."

All three of his children winced simultaneously, but said nothing.

I glanced at my fob watch: three fifty-one. I had nine minutes in which to convince the medical proxy to sign the forms before the room had to be vacated and the procedure abandoned. I couldn't have a black mark against my name for such a simple case, not that early on in my career.

I dragged over a chair and sat beside Mr Furstein, watching as the redness that had cultivated in his cheeks spread gradually across his otherwise colourless face. "Mr Furstein," I said as softly as I was able, "I can't pretend to know what you're going through right now and I know I'll never fully understand how much your wife means to you, but this isn't your wife. This isn't the person you married. You might ask how I could say this, how could I possibly know anything about her when I've only been treating her for a few short weeks?"

His eyes broke away from the bed and hovered towards the floor.

"I know because her brain told me. Her test results told me. Internally your wife has changed so dramatically that comparing a scan of her brain two years ago to one taken today would be like looking at two completely different people. Don't you agree that she's changed? And what's most important is..."

"Did the brain scan show that she's in pain?"

I looked up at the Fursteins' daughter, who had tentatively moved away from the corner of the room. Her body was rigid, and as the tears fell she scrubbed them roughly from her cheeks.

"Pain?" I said. "Not with..."

The daughter shook her head and jutted her chin towards her father, whose gaze was still directed at the linoleum.

I nodded. "Well…yes. It showed that she's in some pain."

Three fifty-five.

"Quite a lot of pain, in fact."

"You see, Dad? Mum needs this. I'm as scared as you are but we need to do this for her before she gets any worse. We can't just leave her to die like this. She's suffering. She's... god, just look at her for Christ's sake, we need to do something."

Watery saliva fell from the old woman's mouth and was absorbed into the bed sheets. It was now three fifty-six, and my hands had clenched into fists.

"But you don't understand," he began.

"I do, Dad. I do understand. She's my mum."

Mr Furstein looked up to his daughter for a few moments, his lips moving silently. Finally he rose shakily to his feet and, expelling a weighted groan, somehow managed to pass his wife without permitting himself another look.

A series of high-pitched bleeps indicated his signatures had been approved on the e-Greement pads. My nails unfurled from my palms.

Now I had to move quickly. I unlocked the cabinet that contained the Coactucin and, with a fresh syringe, pierced the foil lid to withdraw the liquid.

"Okay, Mrs Furstein," I said, walking back to the bed, "in a minute I'm going to give you some medicine that will make you feel a little sleepy."

Three fifty-seven.

I glanced over at the family. "If there's anyone here who wishes to stop the procedure please make your objections known now."

Silence.

Three fifty-eight.

I spoke faster, this time to the patient. "Mrs Furstein, your husband is your medical proxy and has approved this procedure on your behalf due to your advanced dementia. However, if you wish for me to stop please give me some indication now, otherwise I'll administer the Coactucin."

Silence.

But then there was a quiet, guttural noise. It came from the depths of Mrs Furstein's throat and out through her gaping mouth. I couldn't tell whether it was anything more than a gargle – I hadn't detected a precise word - but her pale blue eyes were looking directly into mine and her heavily lined lips twitched at the corners. I looked to the family, but they were huddled together at the other side of the room, heads bowed and hands clasped around each other as if in prayer. Not one of them seemed to have heard her.

Three fifty-nine.

I stabbed the needle into the tubing of Mrs Furstein's IV and pushed the plunger. Her wrinkled eyelids fluttered, her head sank further into the pillow and she became unconscious.

Four o'clock.

The door creaked as one of the sweeps peered into the room. Noting the empty syringe in my hand, he checked his fob watch and scribbled the time onto the device in his hands. He then offered a small bin lined with a plastic bag. I held the syringe over it, hesitating.

*Section 10: Part 5: Even with the use of a medical proxy the euthanasist must attempt to gain firsthand consent for the procedure from the patient, having made him/her fully aware that the administration of Coactucin will result in certain death. If a comprehensible response is given, the procedure must be terminated.*

Comprehensible.

I dropped the syringe.

# 2

Through dirt-spattered glasses Logue stared out at the grounds, his mouth taut in concentration. I briefly considered making conversation but instead settled on looking at the sky through the same scratched and smeared lenses while we waited.

Eventually Doctor Watts swung open the door, flinging about his customary apologies as he unbuttoned his suit jacket to sit at his desk. As head doctor he was the only member of staff with the authority to dismiss standard uniform in favour of the impracticality of a shirt, tie and waistcoat. The rare scent of old money lingered on each garment he wore, but while the suits were a cherished privilege for Watts they were a meaningless vestige of archaic times to everyone else in the facility. That being said, I did find them structurally fascinating.

Once Logue had mustered enough strength to turn his attention away from the window, Watts took his cue and began the meeting.

"I won't keep you for long," he said, resting his elbows on the desk, "I know how busy you both are. I just wanted to discuss the possibility of some changes for the two of you."

My stomach tensed involuntarily, lurching me forward. I looked to Logue but his sagging, dreary face gave nothing away other than the fact that he hadn't shaved for a few days. He either didn't know or didn't care about the subject matter of the meeting. Probably both.

"It's come to my attention," Doctor Watts continued, "that there's been an uneven distribution of patients among the euthanasists at Boar House."

As I hadn't had a patient in over a week and I knew Logue had been juggling two, I permitted my excitement to escalate until it burned the skin of my cheeks.

"Bill, you've been here for what, thirty years now?" Watts asked, to which Logue replied with an imperceptible nod. "It goes without saying that you've played a vital role in building the reputation of the facility to the level it is today and your knowledge and experience is unrivalled. As such, I feel your wisdom could really benefit someone like Nieve, who's only just started out in her career. She's proven herself with the older patients but I think it would be useful for her to shadow you for a while. Maybe she could even take on some of your responsibilities over the next few months. This would be on a trial basis, of course, just so she can gain some practical experience on the more complex cases, but I think it could be an invaluable learning curve. What do you think?"

Logue shifted uncomfortably as Watts and I turned to him, which was understandable since he had more or less been told to accept the beginning of the end of his career. It was widely known that Logue had been displaying the most common retirement symptoms of a euthanasist – a wearied fatigue that had gradually decayed into ineffectualness – and now Watts had assigned a replacement to help nudge him out of the profession completely.

And it was to be me, a young and relatively inexperienced euthanasist, who had been chosen to take over. I had expected some sort of recognition for my recent work but nothing so momentous so soon, especially since Watts was the kind of man who found thanking the cafeteria staff an arduous task. When presented with a tray at lunch he'd just slightly raise one corner of his mouth, as if from him that was worth more than words could ever express.

"I was thinking," Watts said, already impatient for an answer, "that you could start by partnering on a case and go from there. That way you can both see how the other works. After that, seeing that it all goes well, Nieve could take on one of the more challenging cases by herself. We could slowly integrate more work your way, Nieve, and unload a bit more from Bill so he can really focus on driving the department to a better place. How does that sound?"

I nodded. "I can start immediately."

I recoiled at the sound of my own eagerness.

"Bill?" Watts prompted, leaning further forward.

Logue raised his head slightly, like a decrepit old dog that had just realised its name had been called. "Okay."

"It'll give you more time to concentrate on reports," Watts reasoned. "I think I'm right in saying there are only two cases with you at the moment, so perhaps you could collaborate with the newest one. Isn't it a VDA?"

"A suicide?" I hadn't been able to stop the word from leaving my mouth, but Watts somehow managed to retain his smile.

"Nieve, you know that word has no place here."

“Of course. I apologise, Doctor Watts, I’m just a bit surprised. I wasn’t aware Boar House still accepted VDA cases.”

I had completed my final thesis on Voluntary Domestic Aid and had always had a personal interest in what was once dubbed ‘assisted suicide’, but as Boar House was a medium-grade facility in the middle of the countryside those sorts of cases were rare. Around seventy percent of the patients were over the age of sixty.

Watts continued as if there had been no interruption. “The patient has been here for a few weeks now and I think he’s around thirty, but I’m afraid I don’t know much more besides that. What’s his name, Bill?”

“David Myre,” Logue said.

“That’s it, Myre. He came in about three weeks ago. It’ll be a really nice starting point and it’s a case you can really sink your teeth into. VDA cases are never easy but I’m sure Bill can help you out if you ever get stuck.”

Logue had returned to the window again, apparently bored by the subject matter. Or perhaps he was trying to conceal his true feelings about the situation. It was hard to tell.

Watts followed Logue’s gaze. A grimace began to form as he surveyed the long pane of glass that ran across the length of the wall. “I’m being told to get that changed,” he said, nodding to the window.

“Oh?” I replied, feeling bored myself now.

“The whole window has to come out. Health and safety. They want to put in some sort of plastic shield and some metal bars on the outside. I think they’re doing it for every window in the building.”

Watts stood and indicated for Logue and I to follow him, which we both did so reluctantly I wondered how he managed to ignore it. Sighing, he tapped on the glass with a perfectly manicured nail. "Security said all sorts could happen to this, like patients could smash their way out or protesters could smash their way in. They even said something about bombs, but surely no one would be able to get anything up here? The only thing prison bars are going to do is ruin the view."

Watts' office was on the top floor at the front of the building overlooking the grounds, which consisted of thick clusters of trees and miles of dark mossy fields. The only way to the outside world was through security gates made of black iron bars, which curled and twisted to reveal the words 'Boar House Relief Facility' to incoming visitors. Peering through the letters were the dozen or so protesters that milled around each day with placards and painted t-shirts. At that time of the afternoon they were sluggish, their faces placid and chants less severe. One or two were still punching the air and roaring slogans but the majority had clearly had enough for a Thursday afternoon. The security guards walked to and from their posts looking wearily at them all.

"Maybe they're worried about the glass falling on someone," I offered, but both men ignored me.

"There's no reason for us to be worried about the protesters," Watts said, "it's the everyday members of the public we need to be concerned with. We have an essential role in society but the public still views us with the same superstitious fear as they do a morgue or a graveyard. I want our facility to be thought of as a compassionate, caring and successful public service, and to do that we need to show them we're a part of normal life, not a dreaded inevitability. Or even worse, some sort of punishment." Watts touched the glass pane, no doubt imagining his heartfelt speech ringing out to the idiotic people below. "We have to consciously push ourselves to unite with them to be seen with the same importance as a doctor or a nurse, and that's the only reason these protesters are a threat: they rob us of a sense of normalcy. We need to end this controversy they hold over us and become part of their everyday lives."

Logue turned away from the window.

"Do the protesters bother you, Logue?" I asked.

He shrugged. "They have a right to be here, and I suppose rights are more important than being right."

"Either way," I said, "I don't think they have much of a negative impact on the work we do, but I am curious about them. I can't imagine the kind of person who would want to stand out there day in, day out, fighting against something that's not only necessary but actively requested by the patients. I want to know what they're thinking."

Watts smirked. "They don't think, that's the problem. If they knew the importance of the work we do they wouldn't be out there. They dwell on the idea of murder, but I guarantee none of them have witnessed a loved one dying of cancer or slowly deteriorating from motor neuron disease. They're privileged, bored individuals who have never had to suffer a day in their lives."

"But you have?"

Watts' smile thinned. "Frankness is a great quality, Nieve, but I wouldn't push it if I were you."

Outside one of the protesters with a lingering burst of energy held up a banner with the slogan 'Killing criminals is a crime', hopped around for a couple of seconds and then fell back into a rhythmic sway with the rest of the group.

"See that?" Watts said. "Do you see that sign? Everything the protesters do is so pitifully misinformed. If they'd done their research they'd know we don't even admit prisoners here."

"Are we ever going to?" I asked.

He stiffened. "I've heard you're one of the advocates for the criminal policy. But like I've said in the dozens of meetings I've had over the past few months, we're a small facility miles away from the city. If we affiliate with the prisons our reputation would be..."

"We would reach level twelve status. Taking into consideration the size and location of the facility, we couldn't reach that any other way."

Watts leaned back on his heels and sucked in his top lip as he studied me. I had spoken out of turn, but the cautious, middle-aged fool required a shove or two to notice the situation's sense of urgency. It wasn't the catatonic residents that kept the facility topical but the innovative, experimental treatments it held. The creation of the Coactucin drug had revolutionised the euthanising procedure and in the process elevated Boar House from a grade eight to a grade eleven, but that had taken place many years before. Another headlining report was desperately needed before the facility fell off the map once again and the government cut their funding.

As was common after a bout of intense discussion, Watts began to laugh softly to himself as he sat back at his desk. It was a move intended to disarm his opponents. "Although I'm glad to see you're passionate about the subject, there won't be any prisoners joining us here. Not for the foreseeable future."

Continuing to argue was pointless, but we both knew there would come a point when he would have to drastically change his stance or Boar House would crumble – like Logue – into insignificance.

Watts straightened his tie and cleared his throat. "How about the two of you reconvene in a couple of days to start the ball rolling with the new patient? I can imagine there'll be a lot to discuss."

I looked to Logue to confirm but, upon seeing a label protruding from the back of his neck, I realised the top of his uniform was inside-out. There really wasn't a single word I wanted to say to him, and I wanted to hear him say even less.

# 3

During my time at Boar House the staff lived in rows of makeshift cottages at the rear end of the facility. Space was limited, cupboards didn't quite close properly and doors opened in the least rational direction. But as the cottages were assumed to be a temporary solution to the transport ban, the bubbles that appeared under the flooring were ignored and the smells of damp and degrading glue were simply masked with bleach.

Despite the less than desirable living conditions, I enjoyed being so close to the facility. Every day I woke early, mostly because I saw no reason not to, and would head to the Research Hub in the main building to work. The Hub was created with the intention of being the central locale for euthanasists, a sort of mix between a common room and a library, but it was airlessly humid no matter what time of year it happened to be and had a grimy, sticky feel to it, as if there were dust and dirt trapped in-between multiple layers of polish. I was one of the few euthanasists to use it regularly, not because I preferred the thick, warm air to the bitter drafts of my cottage, but because the devices within it had unrestricted access to all resources and patient files. The limitless research was the main reason I had listed Boar House as my employer of choice.

This unrestricted access was a privilege I imagine would make most euthanasists wince these days, and probably with good reason; I often breached protocol by looking through my colleagues' files, either out of curiosity or sheer nosiness, and following my meeting with Watts I thought nothing of reading Logue's notes on our soon to be joint patient, David Myre.

The file on Myre was shockingly minuscule. It definitively stated that the patient was white, male and thirty-two years old, but his height and weight remained unconfirmed and his hair colour was simply labelled 'dark'. He apparently had no distinguishing scars, was a non-smoker and non-drinker, and had no physical conditions other than a mild allergy to tree pollen. No history of clinical depression or other mental illnesses permitted for VDA cases was mentioned, nor was he diagnosed with any unpermitted conditions. He was listed as unemployed but didn't receive state-funded monetary aid, which meant he probably had very rich, very generous relatives.

That being said, David had refused to provide contact details for his next of kin (the national records had been forced to provide his parents' address) so it was possible his family were unaware of his admittance to the facility. It wasn't unusual for VDA patients to exclude their families from the relief process, often due to protectiveness or shame, but it put my theory of being financially supported by rich family members into doubt. If he had relied so heavily on them, surely they would have known about his application?

I scrolled through the pages upon pages of useless, innutritious information, desperate to find something that would help define the case. The file was so nondescript that it could have applied to a million other patients, and since there was no record of illegal misdemeanours, personal tragedies or even the slightest abnormality in his preliminary blood work, I could only conclude that there was no perceptible reason as to why David Myre had submitted himself for voluntary euthanasia.

The only mildly intriguing part of the file was that the psychiatrist who had put David forward for relief had, besides filling out the standard forms required, merely written as her official statement: 'After assessment I can formally conclude that Mr Myre is an ideal candidate for terminal relief and I propose he be admitted to the Boar House Relief Centre upon immediate vacancy.'

That was it. It seemed nothing more than an afterthought.

David Myre was a John Doe with a name. He had boarded at the facility for almost a month without anything significant added to his file, but while I doubted Logue could pick him out of a line-up I could hardly refuse the opportunity to collaborate with him. There was nothing to do other than willingly go down with a sinking ship.

Further research was pointless, so I decided the only rational thing to do was to meet David in person. It took quite a while to find his room, as internally Boar House was nothing but a series of long, thin corridors with few visual cues to differentiate one ward from another. The grey vinyl flooring bled seamlessly throughout the entirety of the building, as did the plain cream walls and harsh artificial light. Occasionally there was a scuff on the floor or some chipped paint that helped to pinpoint where I was, but mostly I had to rely on the map on my e-Noter to get around.

David had been placed at the very end of a row of empty rooms, in-between a fire escape and an area used by the sweeps to store their gurneys. His isolation from the rest of the ward didn't fill me with a great deal of confidence. Perhaps Logue thought if he placed him away from everything he would be forgotten about.

Through the one-way glass panel, I could see the floor in David's room had been buffed so meticulously it looked like a flat pool of water surrounding the bed. The rest of the room was laid out in the standard way for a VDA patient: four silicone storage cubes in the corner for personal effects, windows confined behind sheets of safety plastic, a bed in the centre without a headboard on a soft frame, a dozen or so cameras fixed onto the ceiling and walls, eNoters secured within safety casing and an automatic door without a handle that led to the bathroom.

The storage cubes were empty, and it took me a while before I spotted David lying on the bed with his back to me, his body wrapped in a sheet with only a few strands of thick, black hair protruding from the top. There was no response as I knocked on the door, so I keyed in the code and went in.

A few steps in I hesitated, unsure what I had hoped to achieve by visiting an unconscious patient without any form of preparation. I removed one of the handheld screens from a compartment on the wall and scrolled through the case file to waste some time, wondering how quickly I could retreat while still keeping my self-respect intact.

"Hello."

I immediately dropped the screen, which zipped back into the wall by its retractable wire. David had turned over and was watching me from the bed, his smile no doubt the result of my response.

The bed sheet had fallen down to his waist, revealing a torso that was nothing but a ripple of bones running jaggedly under discoloured skin. His neck, pulsating and writhing with prominent tendons, made way to a thin jaw and hollow cheeks covered in grey, flaky skin. I could see the outline of his eye sockets. He couldn't have weighed more than a hundred and ten pounds.

It was the stark contrast of his inky hair against his natural fairness that attributed most to his colourless, ill appearance. His hair was so dark it could only have been the result of dye – the black tufts just didn't sit right with his pallid complexion.

"Hello?" he repeated.

I forced myself to focus on conversing. "Yes. Hello, David, my name is Nieve Hindeman."

I offered my hand but he didn't take it. It wasn't so much of a snub, he just didn't want to shake my hand.

As he tried to sit up straight he winced and slid back down into a slouch. I imagined there must have been a number of purulent bedsores covering his underside from the look of his weakened body. He must have been bedridden for months – there was no way he was strong enough to stand, let alone walk.

"And how can I help you, Nieve Hindeman?"

"I'm your euthanasist," I said rather more bluntly than I had meant to, trying not to stare at the way his breathing made his ribs undulate beneath translucent skin.

"I could have sworn you were a man last time you visited."

I stared for a second, trying to comprehend what he meant. "Oh, you mean Mr Logue? We'll both be taking care of your case now. He and I will be with you tomorrow afternoon, I just thought I'd introduce myself ahead of that."

"Tomorrow afternoon?"

I nodded. "For your consultation."

"Right," he said, nonplussed.

I admit to feeling a little overwhelmed by that point. His physical state alone would have made a fascinating case study, but there had been no comment, note or even so much as an offhand remark about his weight and general ill health on his file. He was an atypical case, I didn't need any experience in the VDA department to see that, and I had absolutely no idea where to start with him.

I suddenly became aware of the lull in conversation and moved closer to the bed. "So how are you feeling today?"

"I feel fine," he said.

Whenever a euthanasist meets a new VDA patient, it's important for them to uphold conversation in close proximity to gauge any adverse reaction to physical closeness. With David I soon overstepped the average person's boundaries (eleven inches apart), yet there was no counter-movement. This was unusual as younger men submitted for VDA tend to have a lower tolerance to breaches of personal space and are often quick to show irritability or even aggression when feeling physically cornered. David simply stared calmly into the distance, even when I shifted a few inches closer.

"How are you finding Boar House?" I said.

I leaned in a little further.

"It's okay," he said, "you don't have to do that."

"Do what?"

"The other guy did this already. Logue, was it? And you look like you're about to cry."

"I'm sorry, I don't know what you mean."

"The get right in my face, touchy-touchy approach. Logue was practically on top of me at one point and kept squeezing my arm like an inappropriate uncle, waiting for me to complain. After a while he stopped asking me things and backed off as far as he could, so I assumed he had only done it to see what I'd do. I've been to enough therapists to know you guys don't do stuff like that for no reason."

He was astute. "So how many sessions has Logue had with you?" I asked.

"Just two, he met me when I arrived and then spoke to me again a few days later." He paused. "That's not the right answer is it? You're annoyed."

"Not at all."

"You look annoyed."

"Why do you think that?"

He laughed through his nose. His eyes shrunk and became enveloped in dry, creased skin as he smiled. "So what's your name again?"

"Nieve Hindeman. I can show you my profile on my e-Noter if you like?"

"No need," he said, suddenly aware of his bare chest and pulling the bed sheet over himself. It wasn't so much out of embarrassment, he was just being dutiful in removing the veiny flesh from view, as if closing a door or straightening an item on a shelf. "No offence, but I'm not planning on memorising your details, I'm only interested in being dead as soon as possible."

I shrugged off his attempt at emotional manipulation.

"I assume you've been made aware that your physical state needs to be improved before we can make any progress towards your treatment," I said. "We also need to perform some tests and cognitive assessments to make sure you're suitable for the procedure. It could take a matter of weeks, maybe months, but we'll discuss your health and any other issues in greater detail at your consultation."

"My health? What do you mean?"

"You're incredibly underweight, David."

He gave a curt laugh. "So you're going to fatten me up before you kill me."

I could tell he was displaying nonchalance to cover real fear, perhaps triggered by the prospect of progression with his treatment. Either that or I had made him feel self-conscious about his appearance.

"We have to make sure your physical condition is not having an impact on your decision to be here," I told him, "especially since your admittance was voluntary. Once we've ruled that out we can focus on the next step of your treatment."

"Why can't you say the word 'die'?"

I had read shock tactics were a common response from VDA patients to gain control, yet when faced with it in practice I hesitated. I then compensated for my error with indifference.

"Of course I can say 'die', David, but that word has nothing to do with your treatment plan at the moment."

"Procedure, treatment, relief...whatever. I've heard all the buzz words now. Why can't you just say that we're both here because you're going to help me die? Whether that's going to happen before or after you've fattened me up, it doesn't matter, at the end of the day it's the only reason we're talking to each other. I just find it weird that no one here dares to say it."

Death is obviously an obsessive subject with most relief patients, but David's attitude differed from what I had been used to. The elderly patients I treated complained about it, talked of their fear of it, its inevitability, but never before had I encountered a challenging tone.

"Well, it's really quite an emotive and aggressive word, and at Boar House we don't see it..."

"Death is aggressive?"

"To some of the patients the word can be, yes. Some of them feel the term is quite cold and doesn't best describe what they are here for. We relieve people of their pain, whether that be physical, psychological or emotional. This is the Boar House *Relief* Centre. We're trying to understand why you're in pain, David, so we can help to alleviate it for you. We aren't here to end your life, we're here to understand you and help you come to a conclusion that is best for you for the good of your health. This may or may not end with the relief procedure you're referring to, which is why death has nothing to do with your treatment plan right now."

The programmed spiel confidently left my lips, but all I could focus on was his bony, trembling hand as it pulled nervously at a clump of tangled hair. Without correct nutrition those dark tufts would soon separate from his scalp as his protein levels dwindled even further. He was falling apart in front of me.

"Relief," he said, mulling over the word. "I suppose it's relief I want. Just as long as we're clear that relief means I'll be dead."

I nodded, wondering why the two words had such separate meanings for him.

# 4

Logue was unmoving, his head in its usual bowed position. A rush of irritation warmed my face; he was nothing but a lump of souring tissue, and it somehow made it worse to know he recognised his own feebleness. Perhaps he even revelled in it.

"I'll have to report this to Watts," I said.

"Report what?"

I was surprised by the sharpness of his retort. "Three weeks. And nothing. He's so underweight, I really don't see how you can justify ignoring him for so long."

"He wasn't being ignored, I was dealing with it."

"How? He should have had a consultation within the first week of arriving, and we're only doing it now because I pushed for it. How long were you going to make him wait?"

"It's a complex case. We had to rule out a lot of other things before we could start, such as eating disorders and hyperthyroidism."

"According to the phys aids, he was tested and given the all clear from all that within the first three days. What's been happening since?"

"It's a process."

"We don't have time for this. Watts is cutting down on case hours as it is and you haven't even weighed him yet, let alone put him on a nutrition plan. The committee won't even acknowledge the case until he's gained at least fifty pounds."

He replied with a shrug. A nonchalant, childish shrug.

"This is my case too, Logue," I said, deciding to abandon conversation. "The outcome will reflect on me as well."

Out of the corner of my eye I saw him open his mouth to reply and then close it again. He spoke so quickly I almost mistook his words for an exhale. "You should call me Bill."

I sputtered a little in disbelief. As I wiped the saliva from my mouth I gave a few exaggerated nods, hoping that would be the quickest way to end such a bizarre, unprompted request, but it seemed to just spur him on.

"Calling each other by our surnames is just so… I don't know, I just feel… if we're supposed to be working together…"

Finally, choked with embarrassment, he returned to his waking coma.

Preferences on how to be addressed, the colour of one's uniform and general small talk were the sort of matters Logue's generation of euthanasists were far too fixated on. He and his peers had played significant roles in medical history as tireless advocates for relief, opening up doors to a whole new level of professionalism, but they had become nuisances in middle age. They had begun obsessing over the most petty and inconsequential details, and Logue's new-found fastidiousness for social conduct was just another tedious element of this.

I suppose David's consultation was the first time I had properly experienced Logue's ineptitude up close, and I was quite taken aback by the extent of it. Not only was he obstructively disorganised when it came to his general approach to the case, but he was also thoughtless enough to have booked us into the smallest assessment room in the facility, with windows that directly faced the front gates. The protesters were clearly visible outside, as were the transportation vehicles coming in and out, creating an incredibly distracting environment for such an important juncture in the case. The lighting was also poor and it was suffocatingly airless. Within minutes sweat had begun to trickle down my back and collect at the waistband of my trousers.

A mutual barricade of silence was quickly enforced between us, but it didn't last long – soon there was a shuffling, a murmur and a light rap on the door. David had arrived.

Before my brain could process a response, the door was kicked and then pushed open by the weight of two bodies. A psych aid, one of the older ones with dark blond hair and a pointed chin, hobbled into the room with David clinging tightly to his shoulders like a chimp. With an arm wrapped around the patient's middle, the psych aid managed to drag David far enough into the room to grab hold of the back of a chair. David, wide-eyed with unsteadiness, shakily lowered himself to sit.

Logue's face was contorted in what I assumed to be an expression of guilt, but I had no time to deride any pleasure from it. Like him, I had also not appreciated just how weak David was.

In the dimly lit, cupboard-like room, David had an almost bluish grey pallor with dark purple smudges smeared beneath his eyes like war paint. Judging from the obvious muscle deterioration in his legs, his condition must have been the result of months of malnutrition and inactivity, if not years. All I could see were bones, arteries, sinewy, chewed muscles and lumpy, grey organs squirming and trembling within him. He was rotting meat.

"Isn't this cosy," David said breathlessly as he looked about the room. I should have attempted pleasantries but all I could do was stare as David's veins writhed like fat worms beneath a transparent membrane. I had never seen a human being in such an appalling condition outside of a history book.

The lingering presence of the psych aid broke me out of my trance.

"Yes?" I said, bemused by his stares.

"There's nothing for me to sit on."

I looked at the two plastic chairs Logue and I were on, the table in front of us, then to David's chair on the opposite side. "It appears not."

"Shall I go get a chair?"

"Why?"

"Won't I be staying for this?"

"Why would you?"

The psych aid made an odd laugh. "I'm David's lead psychiatric support, I've been working closely with him since the day he arrived."

"Yes, well, of course I'll make sure you're forwarded a copy of the report," I said, indicating towards the door with an outstretched hand.

"I've been in consultations before, I know the drill. Maybe I could…"

"That won't be necessary."

"Have you read my notes?"

My toes gripped onto the soles of my shoes. Phys aids and psych aids often overstepped their boundaries, with many seeming to believe that because they dealt with the patients' day-to-day issues they were somehow fundamental to the overall relief process. In reality they were nothing more than glorified carers.

Thankfully, this psych aid soon appreciated the situation and left, although he closed the door a little louder than was necessary behind him.

"Okay, that was awkward," David said, smiling gleefully to reveal lightly yellowed teeth. The resident dentist must have attempted to clean them but years of neglect had left the enamel permanently stained.

Logue didn't appear to be budging from his vegetative state, so it was up to me to start the session. From the controls on my e-Noter I locked the nine cameras in the room onto David's position, and as they shifted into place they made a low buzzing sound that reverberated deep in my ears. David turned in his seat to look as they followed every minute tilt of his head.

"I suppose that's the cue to start, then," he said. "How many people are watching us right now on those?"

"No one, we're just recording this for future reference."

"Sure."

"With the Confidentiality Act I have a legal obligation to inform you whenever you're being observed. We have a strict code of discretion at Boar House as well as extensive security measures for your privacy and protection, so you needn't worry about anyone listening in outside of this room."

David had already dismissed my words.

I pushed my tongue in between my teeth to stop my jaw from clenching. It wasn't surprising that the pressure I had been feeling was beginning to manifest itself in me physically; this one-hour consultation was my only opportunity to reject the case if I deemed it liable to fail at committee. On the other hand, if I found the case to be workable I had such a narrow timeframe in which to prove it that the likelihood of it failing at committee was uncomfortably high. A failed case so early on in my career would have tarnished my reputation irreparably as, unlike Logue, my past successes were not significant enough to compensate for any future inadequacies.

On top of all that, if David was denied treatment for any reason, and it became publicly known that he had waited almost a month to be assessed, the facility would be investigated for gross misconduct. There would be suspensions, fines and sanctions just so the committee could save face.

I had been forced into a precarious situation due to the incompetence of a colleague, who was likely to emerge unscathed once retired, but I couldn't allow myself to dwell on that side of things. I had to make it work, and as my biggest and most immediate concern was the uncertainty of the situation I decided to begin David's consultation with the most direct question I could think of.

"Why are you here, David?"

He looked to Logue. When Logue failed to reassure him with a returned glance, Davis lifted his palms towards the ceiling. "Well," he replied, "I think the answer to that should be quite obvious."

"All right, but let's pretend I'm your community doctor and you've just come to see me with your application. Why do you want to be put forward for Boar House?"

"To die."

I ignored his blatant attempt to goad me. "Why do you want to do that?"

He looked again to Logue but his pleas for some form of male camaraderie were ignored. "Because I don't want to live."

A pointless, thoughtless retort. He was refusing to engage with me.

"Why?"

"Because I don't."

I had read young male VDAs often tried to dominate or disrupt their own assessments – a pointless trait developed from a self-destructive nature. I had to stamp out this sort of behaviour if I was to find any legitimacy to the case.

"Talk me through the steps that led to your application for Boar House."

"I'd rather talk about the steps that will lead me out of here, to be honest. In a body bag, if you know what I mean." His voice remained flat but he couldn't stop a self-satisfied smile from creeping in at the corners of his mouth.

His attempt at deflective humour was odd. Usually only the able-minded terminal patients would make such candid remarks about their own death. His clumsy jests didn't fit with the typical behaviours of a patient volunteering to end his own life, that much was certain.

I opened his file with the e-Noter. "I see you've been to several therapists over the past five years for fairly brief periods. You experienced mild to moderate symptoms of depression and bouts of apathy during that time. The final therapist you saw sent a request referral for relief treatment after only three sessions, from which point you were sent to the pre-procedural clinic for assessments with Therapist Bolton. He admitted you to Boar House within two days citing dysthymia. That seems very quick."

"I suppose."

"You suppose? Is that what happened?"

"If it's written down then it must have happened."

He wasn't smiling any more, but I could tell he was enjoying himself. Enjoying the attention.

"That's the problem," I said, "it's not all written down. Not in any great detail anyway. I'd like to hear your side of things, just so I can get a better idea of what you've been through and where you're at now. Did anyone explain what will happen during your time here?"

"You talk to me, poke me with psychoanalytical sticks and if it all seems depressing enough it goes to court. Then I die."

I could no longer tell whether he was being facetious or attempting to hide a genuine lack of knowledge. "No, it doesn't quite work like that. Do you know what needs to be achieved before you can get approval for the relief procedure?"

I took the shrug and sudden indifference as an attempt to mask his cluelessness, but his lopsided smile seemed relaxed, knowing and amused. I was having a lot of trouble reading him.

"There will be cognitive sessions," I said, "behavioural assessments, physical examinations and an extensive search into your medical and personal history. This is all to determine whether you're a suitable candidate for relief.

After that, if you're ready I'll present your case report to the Humanitarian Governing Committee, although you'll hear them being referred to as just 'the committee' here. They'll help bring a conclusion to your case, which will either involve the relief procedure or a transfer to a specialist clinic, but we'll cross that bridge when we come to it. Does that all make sense?"

"Yeah, I knew all of that already. I was sent about a thousand documents."

I hesitated, still not quite sure what he was trying to do. "Good."

I let a silence form, but David was unflinching in the face of it, his focus now on the protesters milling about outside. He seemed disinterested and unsettled, but with my lack of experience I found his behaviour difficult to interpret.

"How are you finding the facility so far?" I asked.

"The food is terrible. The mashed potato tastes powdery and there's only about four different dishes served at dinner. Last week I had sausage and mash two days in a row. And I'm a bit sick of toast for breakfast and sandwiches for lunch, can't they serve anything other than bread for two out of the three meals? On pizza days I have three meals with bread in it and it's a bit much, you know?"

I nodded – the food served at Boar House was notoriously uninspiring, but a repetitious menu was deemed by many experts as an essential part of a healthy patient's routine.

"I actually meant in terms of support from the staff, but seeing as we're on the subject, what has your appetite been like recently? Do you think you're eating more here than you did at home?"

"I suppose."

"Why do you think that is?"

"I don't know."

"To get so underweight you must have starved yourself for a very long time. It must have been a painful experience to go through."

"Not really."

"Why did you stop eating?"

"I don't know."

"You'll be going on a tailored nutrition plan soon, how do you feel about that?"

"Fine. Whatever you want."

I was becoming increasingly frustrated. With only seventeen weeks to complete the case there was no way I could leave the first consultation without something to go on, no matter how minuscule that something happened to be, and David seemed prepared to fight me all the way.

The warm, recycled air was like congealed saliva coating my skin.

"Let's go through what we already have," I said, trying to read the e-Noter as my vision quivered. "It says here you achieved a basic level of education. When you left school you were assigned to a grade nine employer and remained there until you were automatically dismissed during your application for Boar House. Your banking records show your job covered your rent but the majority of your finances were dealt with by an anonymous benefactor."

"So? None of that matters now, does it?"

"Actually it's quite relevant for our investigation into your background. Do you feel comfortable telling me who your benefactor was?"

"Why don't you just look at my accounts and find out?"

"We only have partial access to them, didn't anyone tell you what we have access to when you were being admitted?"

"I must have tuned out."

"I see. Well, there's certainly a lot of information to process while being admitted, so that's understandable. But to go back to my earlier question, could you tell me anything about your benefactor? What was the arrangement there? Do you feel you've struggled with money a lot in your life?"

He sighed and looked up to the ceiling. "Any reason why you're asking me this?"

"We need to establish your past before we can proceed with your future. Knowing more about your life will help us figure out how to tackle your case. So, if you could answer the question: has money ever been an issue for you? Who supplied you with food? And with money for your bills?"

He waited a while before shaking his head. "You're going to make this a really boring conversation. There's not much to say."

My vision began to narrow as the heat of the room swelled. I wasn't getting anywhere. I reluctantly let go of the subject and scrolled through my notes, desperately trying to find something, *anything*, that would pacify my increasing sense of doubt about the case.

And then, in the midst of the nothingness, an anomalous, overlooked detail. A visitation request.

David had invited a Mr Trent Williams to visit, although the request form had sat abandoned on the file since his admittance. Logue hadn't even managed to gather the visitor's details let alone arrange a pass for him.

"Who's Trent Williams?" I asked.

And right there, with that one sentence I had it; the beginning of something. His eyes snapped downward and his shoulders fell, if only for a moment, but I had seen it. I rolled my sleeves up, feeling the cool air beginning to lick at my arms.

"Who's Trent Williams?" I asked again.

"A friend."

"How did you meet?"

"It doesn't matter."

"I think I'll be the one to decide what matters, David."

Logue twitched in his chair, but I determined his scowl to be the result of an involuntary motor function and ignored him.

I leaned back, stretched my legs out in front of me and folded my arms in a dominant posture. "If you're not going to talk to me why did you bother to come here?"

"I'm talking to you right now, aren't I?"

"I'm asking simple questions and your answers have been incredibly vague. It's only going to get more invasive as we progress with the case, so if you won't answer me now how is it going to be in a few weeks' time? If you want my help you need to give me something to work with."

"I don't know why this is so hard for you to understand," he grunted, mirroring my pose with his skeletal arms."I came here because I want you to inject me, simple as that, so what else is there to say?" He looked to the window as a MediTaxi eased past the small crowd of protesters and through the opening gates. "I'm very bored of this conversation now."

"The quicker you answer me, the quicker we can be finished with the session."

He propped his head up with his hands and continued to follow the MediTaxi.

"At least answer one question. Just one. Will you do that for me?"

David didn't move.

"Why exactly do you want to die?"

Of course I had used the word solely for effect, but the only thing it managed to do was pull Logue from his vegetative state. He cleared his throat in warning.

The famous quote from Dr Hanfield came to mind: 'If you cannot determine grounds for treatment within ten minutes, the case will either take your time or your name.'

I could afford neither option.

"The time is two thirty-six," I said, closing my e-Noter and pushing my chair back. "Mr Logue, I think I'm going to submit an emergency review for this case."

"Is that wise?" he asked, although his voice didn't convey much concern.

"Yes," I replied, and when Logue gave no further comment I stood and began to gather my things.

David gripped onto the desk and shakily pulled himself up to stand. "What's going on? What do you mean?"

"I'm going to set up an emergency review," I kept my voice as even as I could manage. "It means I'll be electing an impartial colleague to help me assess your case to see whether we should continue or not. So far you've been reluctant to communicate, some might even say disinterested, and there's reason to believe you'll remain uncooperative. At present you don't show any signs of someone who will progress successfully or benefit from the procedure."

"I don't understand, what does that mean for me?"

"If we can't find any definitive evidence that you should be a patient here within the next forty-eight hours, you'll most likely be transferred."

"You can't do this, I've been here for weeks. I saw dozens of doctors to get here. You can't just do this after one fucking meeting!"

"It's my duty as a euthanasist to ensure..."

"Yes, fine, I get it, just tell me what I need to do."

I put my bag back down on the table, feeling both fascinated and disturbed as the light illuminated spidery blue veins beneath the crinkled skin of David's forehead.

"You get it? What do you mean? Get what?"

He allowed himself to slide back down onto his chair. "What do you need to know for me to stay?"

Logue was fidgeting uncomfortably in his seat like a dog pawing at the door to be let out.

"I want to know how we can help you, David."

"What does that mean?"

"You need to start telling me about yourself."

He nodded and swallowed. "Well, I..."

A large crackle and a high-pitched whine dissolved his words.

"Choose life not death!"

Outside the protesters had moved away from the gates, all except for one tall, thin man with a megaphone pressed against his lips.

“Kill the pain, not the patient!” he yelled, rattling the gate with his free hand. “Choose life not death!”

A few protesters joined in half-heartedly, but most were backing away slowly, their attention fixed on the security guards circling nearby.

“Choose life not...ah fuck...”

The megaphone was yanked out of the man’s hand by a fat uniformed guard. After a pathetic struggle he was pushed to the ground and the guard sat on top him. The guard then spoke wearily into his handheld radio for backup.

David began to snigger.

“I think that’s enough,” Logue said, leaning forward to close the blinds.

I nodded, trying to unstick the dampened uniform from my body. There was no sense in continuing now, everything had been ruined. I began packing up my things again.

David’s smile vanished. “So what’s going to happen to me now?”

I sighed. “I suppose we’ll push the emergency review aside for the moment.”

“So I’m staying?”

“For the moment.”

“Okay,” he said, nodding, “thank you.”

But I wasn’t doing it for him. He had simply been at Boar House too long. Whether I thought he was viable for relief or not, I had no choice but to accept him as my patient.

# 5

James Turner himself taught me during the first year of my studies. When *Turner's Law of Separation* was released five or so years later, it was strange reading it knowing I had spoken directly to its creator, the research and theories reaching my ears and the ears of my classmates before anyone else in the world.

I distinctly remember typing the first words he spoke onto the back page of my textbook: 'Don't believe what you hear; we euthanasists are not murdering monsters. Our ability to do what we do is not down to coldness or lack of care, but sterility of the mind. Unnecessary sympathies are overwhelming and corrode like disease until you're left with nothing, and your patient even less.'

Of course, his various quotes and methods are now well-known, perhaps even a little outdated, but back then he was regarded as not only a brilliant mind but a revolutionary. He was the first to openly reject the sense of shame euthanasists had been encouraged to feel, as if their guilt was somehow a necessary element to the task at hand. He helped the profession move beyond its moral stagnation, although the public have yet to catch up.

For me, Turner's most memorable lecture concerned his late mentor, the infamous Doctor Alexander Verne. Otherwise known as 'Uncle Alex' by the press, Verne was known to attend patient funerals and would write to their families for months afterwards. It truly was a different era back then.

"He had one patient," Turner had said, walking slowly up and down the stage of the auditorium, "who sticks out most vividly in my mind. Let's call him 'Adam' since he was my first test subject for the *Law of Separation*. Adam was a thief and a liar and had alienated himself from his family by causing countless disputes. He exploited his parents' good nature on a regular basis and intimidated women in an aggressive and sexual way, to the extent that he was only seen by male members of staff by the end of his treatment. On the whole he was selfish, hostile and awkward to be around. He definitely seemed to have a general dislike for the human race.

"Adam claimed that he wanted the procedure for two simple reasons: one," Turner raised a solitary finger in the air, "because no one else wanted him around him, and two," he raised a second finger, "because he didn't enjoy being alive. To paraphrase, he once said to me, 'It would be best for everyone if I just didn't exist'."

Turner often allowed the room to stew in silence while his thoughts aerated. He wouldn't utter a word until he could feel every member of the audience positively twitching with anticipation. Critics accused him of being a showman but I saw nothing negative in his delivery. The whole point of it was for his students to retain his teachings, which was clearly a resounding success.

He eventually began to speak again, slowly and deliberately. "Whenever Doctor Verne sat down with Adam's mother she became hysterical. She gave him a list of reasons why Adam should be denied the procedure and claimed he was in need of another type of help, but she was ignored because Verne decided she had a variation of Stockholm syndrome after years of psychological and emotional abuse. He ignored her attempts to intervene and even dismissed my own words of concern, claiming I didn't know any better as I was but an inexperienced student." Turner smiled playfully to titters from the audience. "With his authority in Lynchfield, Verne was able to quicken Adam's treatment process. Many physical and psychological tests were hurried or skipped entirely simply because he felt a nice woman had been suffering at the hands of her horrid son. 'A mother's love can overpower reason', he had said to me."

Turner stopped again, looking around the auditorium with an expression that suggested the story would have a grave ending. I remember looking at the fascinated faces around me drinking in every droplet of information. Turner was showing us a glimpse of our future, telling us the kind of difficulties we would have to face within a few short years. He had seen the worst cases and was desperate for us not to repeat those mistakes.

Turner dropped down and sat on the edge of the stage. "Well," he said, shaking his head, "the procedure was accepted two weeks after admittance. Fourteen short days. Neither before nor since has a VDA case been processed so quickly. Who would have doubted the great Doctor Alexander Verne? No one. He hadn't followed protocol because he *felt* he was doing the right thing, and no one else followed protocol because everyone trusted his judgement and *felt* he knew what he was doing. The pentobarbital was practically forced down Adam's throat and he died with his mother and father weeping by his side. It wasn't until six months later, as Verne was being investigated for other misconducts, that Adam's records were properly assessed by the committee. Does anyone know what they found?"

A few hands were raised but Turner nodded for them to be lowered again. "Good, and I don't want the rest of you to forget this either. The committee discovered that Adam had been in the process of being diagnosed with an antisocial personality disorder eight years before and, as we all know, it is illegal to provide relief for this sort of condition. Verne, because he felt he knew best, had either hidden this information from those involved – myself included – or simply didn't look into the medical history thoroughly enough. He was therefore a murderer of a very mentally unwell young man."

There were sighs and mutterings of disapproval among the students. The word 'murder' had been heartily adopted by the protesters and was therefore treated delicately by those in the profession, but Turner had said it boldly and without hesitation.

"The renowned Doctor Verne was later imprisoned and became the first person to request relief on criminal grounds. His relief was granted in London fourteen years ago, which devastated me at the time, but it proves to me now that the system is untouchable if we all work towards maintaining its integrity.

"However tragic this story may be, we must remind ourselves that it is because of Doctor Verne that we are now able to help hundreds of criminals every year. It is because of Doctor Verne that we have healthy euthanasist-patient relationships. It is because of Doctor Verne that we are comfortable with our place in society. In a way, he unknowingly sacrificed himself for the benefit of hundreds and thousands of people. Maybe even millions. It's now up to you to carry out a job that not many people could do, not even the great Doctor Alexander Verne, but I believe in you. I believe you can rectify past mistakes and most of all, I believe you can bring peace to those who need it the most."

The applause made my ears ring for hours afterwards.

That day Turner taught me that the blood, bones and matter of the patient is all that's needed to make the right decision, no matter what the circumstances. He talked about absorbing oneself in the process rather than the patient, for misplaced emotions cause mistakes. The same can be said for misplaced apathy, which Logue was undoubtedly guilty of.

Turner also taught me what it meant to be a euthanasist. I wasn't a doctor, carer, therapist, social worker or friend – the patients had other people to turn to for those needs – I offered something uniquely different.

Defining the important work of euthanasists to the general public has always been hard, particularly when it comes to VDA patients. If a VDA patient isn't physiologically unwell but still requests relief, how can the outcome be regulated? If there are no definitive tests, how can we know that the process is being carried out for the right reasons?

That was the problem; no euthanasist ever knew whether they were making the right decision. For a long time, VDA specialists used a mixture of experience, instinct and research to conduct their work, but Turner inspired a need within me to create a method that would add tangibility to my profession. Not long after the lecture

I began to form a theory that I believed would revolutionise Voluntary Domestic Aid cases, a theory I called desistance.

I've always been fascinated by tissue growth and how it transforms to protect the body. Scars usually look delicate despite their violent origins, and my own, formed by a booted foot crushing my fingers into tarmac, are a soft and silvery white with hints of baby pink. Although the fingers themselves are bent, calloused and ugly, the scars are simple and smooth.

While in hospital I studied my splintered fingers as they strengthened, the cuts as they shrank and the scabs as they stiffened and flaked away. The tender, raw flesh beneath was so clear and so perfect that it seemed perverse for these young cells to be surrounded by older, flawed skin. I wondered if my scars were of a similar composition to the new, delicate flesh of a foetus.

It turned out I was wrong. During training I learned the biological distinction between scar and foetal tissue, yet I found my thinking could be applied to psychological scarring; after a traumatic event, established logic is torn away and in its place young, primal thoughts start to form. From then on, whenever the root cause of that mental scar is broached, rudimentary instincts and a desire for comfort consume the brain – simply put, trauma replaces an adult's rational logic with the innate reactions of a child.

Are there ways of healing psychological scars? Yes, if the individual can relearn the thought processes that were lost to the trauma, but this usually requires a certain level of mental strength. It's like saying in order for a damaged car to be fixed it must first drive to a garage, but the more in need of repair the car is the less likely it will be able to get there. Sometimes a car just can't be fixed.

Sometimes a person can't be fixed either.

The idea that relief is the only medical option for some patients is broadly recognised and accepted in the profession, but how can you accurately diagnose someone to be psychologically terminally ill?

I conducted a great deal of research outside of my normal studies and eventually noticed a set behavioural pattern in successful VDA patients. The state the individuals reached when suitable for relief, which I dubbed desistance, had symptoms that included general slow reaction to stimulus, impassiveness and absolute cooperation. In the past, this sort of behaviour was colloquially referred to as the acceptance stage of Kübler-Ross's five stages of grieving, but I don't believe it to be a state of acceptance but rather a cessation of the survival instinct.

Over ninety-five percent of the patients I researched showed some form of desistance by the date of their relief. The five percent of patients who hadn't were arguably failed cases (there were discrepancies, questionable decisions and in some cases full-blown negligence in these reports).

It may have been nothing more than a theory, and a premature one at that, but if I was right, desistance would completely change the face of euthanasia. It would bring a higher degree of certainty to all cases, ridding the profession of hacks like Logue and outlining the need for scientific accuracy over emotional involvement.

And I had found the case that would start it all. David was to be my Adam.

# 6

A few days after David's first consultation, Watts asked me to observe Logue as he performed the relief procedure for his other patient. Watts claimed it was for educational purposes, but I felt more like a chaperone than a student.

I was to witness the first procedure Logue had performed in fifteen weeks, prior to which two of his cases had failed at committee and another had been transferred to a psychiatric facility with overlooked symptoms of a curable mental illness. The patient I was to observe had been approved by the committee some weeks before, so it was unlikely Logue could mess it up at such a late stage.

Despite arriving early, the equipment had already been laid out, the preselected music was being played (some sort of elevator jazz) and the patient was dressed in the mandatory dark green gown. The room was one of the larger ones on the ground floor to accommodate for the patient's special medical needs, but as Logue, the patient and the patient's wife were all close to the bed, the room looked enormous – almost to the point of absurdity.

Logue was leaning over the patient, his mouth hovering just above his ear. As I opened the door he patted him on the back of the hand and took a step back.

"Bill?" the patient's wife said, giving me such a look of alarm I faltered a little.

Logue smiled at her – a rarely seen expression on him. It made his big, droopy eyes shrink inwards as the folds on his face bunched together. He looked subhuman, almost lizard-like.

"May," he said, "this is Miss Nieve Hindeman. She's another euthanasist here."

The woman stared at me incredulously. "I don't know who she is, why is she here?"

I held myself back from relaying protocol to her. Technically I could have made her leave, but as I was to do no more than observe I allowed Logue to handle it.

He made his way around the bed to Mrs Buchanan, giving her shoulder a gentle squeeze. She replied by resting her hand on his. "Remember what I said, May," he said. "Remember what I said to focus on. These little things, these little changes and unforeseen problems, they don't matter. We can't predict everything and unfortunately your husband's procedure has to be observed by another euthanasist for reasons not worth going into now. It's just not important. We've got one person to think about today and that's your husband, everything else is nothingness."

The woman nodded and gulped down a couple of breaths. I found her unwavering trust in him incredibly disturbing.

Logue walked passed me, nodding his head towards the door. I followed him out. As soon as the door closed behind me he spoke low and fast, the dry, crusted saliva in the corners of his mouth cracking and flaking with the movement of his lips.

"I don't think it's best for you to be here right now," he said. "This is final stage, you won't learn anything from watching me now. You'll get far more out of the Myre case."

"Doctor Watts specifically told me to report on this."

"Maybe you could observe from out here? You'll be able to see everything, and you could link your e-Noter up to the audio to hear what's being said. It's just…this is a sensitive time and they're clearly quite distressed."

"No, the patient's wife is distressed, which isn't of any concern to us. Mr Buchanan was the one to have requested the procedure and probably doesn't want it to be drawn out by pointless rhetoric."

Logue placed his fingers round the door handle, gripping so hard his knuckles went white."If I could just speak to May first, I..."

"I don't see why that's needed. The procedure is scheduled to be completed in twenty minutes and as your colleague I suggest you use your time wisely. You can just pretend I'm not here. I won't say a word or interfere unless expressly asked."

He sucked in his teeth and scowled, but the moment he stepped back into the room his exasperation dissipated. I perched on the table at the back of the room, intrigued to see what would unfold.

After a few final checks, the wife insisted on speaking on behalf of her husband, whose slow, blinking eyes tracked her as she read from a battered handheld. She spoke of their children and how they hadn't wanted the relief procedure to tarnish their memories of him, hence their absence, and how their one-year-old grandson would be told stories of Mr Buchanan every single day so he knew the sort of man he had been. They would all keep him in their hearts and never forget him, not even for a single moment.

I've always wondered how long grief actually lasts. After overcoming a new routine and a few initial bouts of nostalgia, how long do people remind themselves to feel miserable before they are able to move on? How do they know when it is socially appropriate to relieve themselves of such an arduous and pointless chore? Is it when everyone around them has demonstrated boredom of the subject? Until they forget? Or do they genuinely remember their relative every day, continuing to self-flagellate in order to fulfil a voluntary, futile duty of remembrance?

The families I worked with always felt the dead wanted to be remembered, but this couldn't have been further from the truth. I saw it in Mr Buchanan's eyes; he wished he were dead, not just because of the pain and the frustration and everything that came with ALS, but because it was exhausting to be around those who were grieving for you before you even had the chance to die. You're never supposed to witness a jury discus your crimes or an ex-partner deal with the aftermath of your breakup, and you're certainly not supposed to see loved ones grieving for you while you're still alive. It's uncomfortable and burdensome, and I can't imagine the pain of politely sitting through that entire process. Luckily, when the time comes I will not have my decrepit elderly mother, an obligated partner, anxious children or bored grandchildren to contend with, just a dependable fellow euthanasist. I will not have to worry about putting on a brave face, trying to give my family a lovely lasting memory through the suffering, or feel the embarrassment as they closely monitor my body while it fails bit by bit. I can scream and kick and shout as much as I want at the unfairness of dying, because my death will be *mine*. They never should have allowed families to watch the procedures like some kind of absurd entertainment.

"Harry," Logue said. The wife had finished her speech and was clasping onto the poor man's deadening claws as she wailed. "Because your wife is your medical proxy and because of the discussions you had with me when you were healthier, you have been approved for relief from your suffering of amyotrophic lateral sclerosis. If you wish to discontinue please blink twice now, otherwise I'll administer the Coactucin."

The man's eyes slowly closed. My stomach gripped to my ribs – but he didn't open them again. It wasn't the first of two blinks, it was his last.

Logue injected Mr Buchanan. As the drug began to take effect his eyes fluttered open, but the shimmer in them had gone. Moments later Logue pronounced him deceased.

The sweep fumbled in, holding out the bin like a lethargic beggar. Once the needle hit the bottom he nodded to each of us in the room, including Mr Buchanan, and went to loiter outside for the body to become available. A psych aid came to take a weary Mrs Buchanan to the family room a short while after.

In one swift, practiced motion, Logue closed the patient's eyelids and lifted the bed sheet over his head.

"Well done," I said, looking at my fob watch. "That was impressive. Great timing."

"Are you being serious? Just get out."

He looked small, crouching beside the covered corpse with his head in his hands, but his voice still had enough spite to echo around the room.

I couldn't understand his protectiveness over a corpse. The hard part was done. Bodies are just meat, empty and useless. It's nothing but a waste product, as significant as a large pile of faeces, yet no matter how much society rejects the church and its practices, the remnants of religion and its effigies are still held dear. We are logical enough to realise that the world was not created in seven days but not quite logical enough to realise that a corpse is just a corpse. A lump of animal meat is cooked and the flesh torn from the bone and consumed, but we pamper our dead, dress them and talk to them like dolls. They are as alive as a doll, as useful as a doll, as meaningful as a doll.

"Didn't you hear me? I want you to get out," Logue said, standing up to face me. He took a couple of steps closer but I could see he had no idea what to do next, his eyes dancing around the room as he looked for a tool, a prop, a word, a thought.

"Don't ruin it," I said, taking a step forward myself.

"Ruin it?"

"Yes. You seemed to be settling back into reality just a few moments ago. You did some good work for the first time in months, now look at you."

He made an odd chuckle. "You think this is reality? That this is good work?"

"Yes. Mr Buchanan needed relief and you gave it to him. It's what he wanted."

"This isn't anyone's first choice. No one wants to die."

"He requested it, he wanted relief."

"And how would you even know the first thing about what he wanted? You've never been outside of these walls. You're a malformed foetus, Nieve, a plant that hasn't been given enough light, you haven't a clue about anything around you. What you think of as normal is just fucked. Do you even have any friends? Family? Does any human being actually choose to spend time with you? You will never understand people and you certainly will never know what they want."

I wanted to reply, I wanted to project a concoction of words like vile sputum and spit it in his face, but every sentence I tried to say sounded feeble and childish.

"Look, I don't want to speak like this in here, not in front of him," he said.

I looked to the bulky mass on the bed and, out of sheer embarrassment for both Logue and for myself, I left.

For over an hour I walked and waited for the anger to evaporate from me, as all emotions tend to do. As all people tend to do. One day Logue will disintegrate and rot and no one will know of him and he will be nothing but flakes of dust. And not long after that I will be nothing but flakes of dust.

The thought calmed me.

* * *

At first the only way I could get to know David without Logue's presence was by observing the daily cognitive sessions he had with his psych aid. I went for the first time a couple of days after the Buchanan case, and I'd being lying if I said my decision to go wasn't inspired by Logue's behaviour after the procedure. It was like an incredibly tame and constructive form of rebellion.

The rooms the psych aids used for these tests had adjoining viewing galleries that could seat up to ten people. The first time I went it was empty, so I sat front row centre, barely a metre from the one-way glass. In the windowless, square room opposite, David was sat at a table with his psych aid, the dark blond one with the pointed chin, who was typing up the results of the Beck scale onto his handheld. David was staring at nothing in particular and tapping the floor with the heel of his foot.

"You know, you've given the exact same score to all of these questions since you arrived," the psych aid said. "It's perfectly fine to rate your mood a five out of ten if that's how you feel, but I'm starting to think that's not the case. Is your answer always a five because you feel okay, because you feel a bit numb or because you're not sure how to score?"

The cognitive tests were used to measure progress and to give another layer of statistics to please the committee, but essentially they were futile activities created to fill up the patient's day and stop them from becoming restless or dwelling too much on the more significant assessments. Of course the psych aids took them very seriously, sometimes writing reports that were thousands of words long, but no one ever read them. No one except other psych aids.

David stretched back, sighing, the individual bumps of his ribs showing through the thin material of his t-shirt. "Don't know."

The psych aid gave a little condescending grin. "Come on, tell me how you really feel right now. Let rip. This is your chance to say anything you want."

"I just feel the same," David said.

"The same as what?"

"The same. I don't know, you're the expert. You figure it out."

The psych aid smiled again. "Okay, Dave, if you're not up for a chat let's move on."

"David, David, David, for god's sake call me David."

"Sorry. Of course, David."

The arrogance was drained from the psych aid in seconds like a burst boil, and his eyes blinked rapidly at the e-Noter as he tried to find whatever it was he was looking for. He flinched as David began to tap the table top with his knuckles.

"So yesterday we talked about catastrophizing,"the psych aid said, his voice now noticeably quieter.

"No, you talked about that. I think I just said it sounded like a made-up word."

The psych aid gave a hollow laugh. "Yes, well I explained what the term means yesterday and today we're going to discuss whether you think it relates to you or not."

"It doesn't. Next topic?"

The psych aid couldn't quite bring himself to laugh politely at that. "Could you think of a time where you may have overreacted to something? Where afterwards you felt the situation wasn't as bad as you originally thought it was?"

"No."

"I have, quite a few times. I think it's natural, especially if we're feeling bad for other reasons. Last week I got soaking wet from the rain because I couldn't unlock the main door to the building. The mechanism was broken, and when tech support managed to get me inside I found out my shift had been changed and I wasn't needed for another four hours. I got very angry and upset and took it quite personally, but looking back it wasn't a big deal at all. I just had wet clothes and was early for work. A few things had simply built up gradually over time and I catastrophized the situation. Does that make sense?"

"No, not really."

"Why not? What about that doesn't make sense for you?"

"Neither of those things were your fault. Your day was messed up because other people are morons, there isn't a single person who could walk away from that singing and dancing. You didn't overreact at all. In fact, I think it would be unhealthier if you weren't angry."

The psych aid considered this for a long time before shaking his head. "No, I don't agree. It would have been okay to be a little annoyed because of the inconvenience and discomfort I was feeling, but to take the whole thing personally was an overreaction. It wasn't a personal attack on me. I jumped to the conclusion that it was all targeted at me, when of course it wasn't."

"But whoever's in charge of your shifts didn't bother to tell you about the changes they made. They must have known that you would turn up to work at the wrong time, which makes it a personal attack."

"It was an honest mistake that anyone could have made, it wasn't done on purpose. Surely you can see that?"

"How do you know?"

"How do I know what?"

"That it wasn't a personal attack? Maybe whoever changed your shift did it out of spite. Maybe you annoy them. Maybe they're trying to piss you off like you piss them off."

I knew exactly what was going to happen next. The psych aid was going to change from his approach as cognitive behaviorist to counselor in order to move the conversation away from himself, and for this particular psych aid that meant changing his actual demeanor. It was as if he adopted a new character, one that was more laidback with sweeping arm movements and a gentler voice. It was excruciating to watch, like a play performed unconvincingly yet passionately by an amateur dramatist.

"So, David," he said in a soft, hushed tone that put my teeth on edge, "let's focus on your childhood for a minute."

It was so laughably cliché.

"Were you a happy child?"

"No."

"Why was that?"

"Being a kid is awful, isn't it?"

"Is it?"

"Yes."

"Why is that?"

David rolled his eyes. "Are you really asking me that? Other kids are horrible. School is boring. You have no freedom. You have to live with your parents. You can't go anywhere or do anything at all so…"

"So have you gone anywhere or done anything as an adult?"

David wilted and began to pick at his nails. Maybe I had underestimated my colleague.

"Dave?"

"Stop calling me fucking Dave, okay? That's not my fucking name."

A prickling sensation went through my body. I opened up the memo section of my e-Noter and wrote: 'No initial symptoms of desistance – quick responses where there should be slow reaction to stimulus, strong reactions where there should be impassiveness, and defiance where there should be absolute cooperation.'

My memory may not be wholly accurate here, but I believe that was the point when I knew David shouldn't have been at Boar House.

# 7

Logue had made sure he was well and truly off the radar after the Buchanan case. I don't know how the man managed to hide himself in a facility as small as Boar House, but he often disappeared for days, sometimes remaining unfound for weeks. His veterancy and an excuse of paperwork seemed sufficient enough to delay any formal investigation.

While Logue may have been able to do as he pleased, Watts expected me to bear the brunt of his work, which meant receiving David's WORM report completely unaided. It was the first of many tasks I had to perform alone.

The WORMs, or Warranted Officers of Residential Materials, were independent investigators hired by relief facilities to accumulate information on complex case files. They were usually retired police or army officials who researched into the lives of patients beyond their digital footprints, interviewing friends and family, examining belongings and determining habits and routines to provide a comprehensive behavioural report. Although these reports were considered anecdotal evidence by the committee, the information was fundamental in determining a focal point for the case. The job is now obsolete, and modern-day euthanasists tend to downplay the WORMs' role within the industry, but they were undoubtedly an essential part of its evolution.

I always found the WORMs useful but despised having to deal with them. They were inexplicably resistant to protocol and it was difficult enough to get them to write their name on the reports, let alone fill in the endless pages of security paperwork required for each patient. Not only that, but as they were classified as external services I was forced to chaperone them for however long they remained on the premises, which meant waiting for them outside at the front gates while they waded through a sea of overexcited protesters.

"Looking for someone?"

I tried to peer through the iron bars but grinning faces and waving hands obscured my view. There was a scattering of laughter as I sighed, my irritation already obvious.

"Do you get paid for standing around with us or do you just get commission?"

"Yeah, how much do you get? Is it more for kids? How much for babies?"

Calls of agreement rose up. A few security guards shuffled from side to side, looking for the subtle warning signs of escalation.

"How many have you murdered? Ten? Twenty? A hundred?"

This question is often thrown at euthanasists, and its repetition perplexes me. I managed to spot the woman who had asked it, a small thin thing with flat hair and a t-shirt saying 'Murder is not medicine' over her small, braless breasts. Why did I need to remember the number of those I had helped? Who would it benefit to hold dear a tally chart of names and statistics? Do doctors ever retain the total number of people they have saved, or even the number of those they have lost?

Before I could form an imagined retort the two WORMs had pushed their way to the front of the crowd. The male WORM, sixty-something and sporting a stained government uniform with a grazing of a beard, wordlessly pushed two ID cards and an e-Greement pad through the bars. I read and scanned them both before taking his and his female companion's fingerprints on the e-Noter. The identities of Marvin and Lane Clarke were quickly confirmed and I punched the code into the gate to let them in.

I was familiar with the professional reputation of this husband and wife WORM team, but their appearance was not quite what I had pictured. As the gates began to open, a tall man with multiple chins concealing all visibility of a neck sidestepped through, followed by a woman with uncontrollable, wiry eyebrows and long grey hair that hung limp about her face. They both shared a look that could only be described as aggressive resignation.

The crowd began to plead with the Clarkes' to turn back but the noise quickly dissipated once the security guards had merged to form a human barrier. All eyes were on the prominent tasers resting on their belts, which allowed the WORMS and I to walk away without any further challenges.

As we made our way down the gravel driveway I tried to match my pace to the Clarkes', but no matter how much I slowed they were always two steps behind.

"I hate all this rigmarole," Marvin mumbled. I turned back to nod in agreement but he looked straight through me, indicating I was not obligated to humour him with insincere politeness. We continued in silence.

To enter the facility there were more security measures to contend with. The ID cards and e-Greement pad were required once more to scan on the door, as were the WORMs' fingerprints. Once I had tapped in the code and scanned my own fingerprints, we were finally admitted into the lobby – from which point the secretary spent around fifteen minutes assigning the WORMs their day passes. Marvin's face began to redden, his cheeks inflating and deflating with increasing speed at each passing second. Lane remained expressionless.

By the time we reached the meeting room Marvin had beads of sweat pricking up through his skin like enlarged, glistening pores.

"Thanks for coming," I said, inviting them to sit. The unforgiving white lights gave the room a clinical ambiance similar to that of the basement morgue.

"Such a pain in the arse every time we come here," Marvin said.

"Yes, my apologies, but it can't be helped."

I pushed forward the e-Greement pad to be signed, which was routine before the delivery of a WORM report. Marvin pushed it back.

"Where's the bloke?"

"Bloke? What do you mean?"

Marvin enunciated each word as if English wasn't my first language. "The man. The man that hired us."

"You were hired by Boar House."

"There's a bloke though. A bloke."

"You mean Logue?"

"Yeah, him, he's supposed to be in charge of this."

"He has other patients to tend to, so I've taken over for this case for now," I said quickly, not having prepared any other form of excuse. I pushed forward the e-Greement and pointed to the two rectangles at the bottom of the page. "So if you and your wife could just sign here, please."

"How do we know this is all above board?"

"You could read the contract through if you want."

Marvin grunted and made a rough squiggle in both boxes. I decided not to press for his wife's signature.

Lane picked up her bag from the floor and dropped it onto the table. She began rifling through the contents and after a while produced a small memory card and a large paper book that she gave to her husband.

The book had a cool grey cover and shockingly white pages with faint blue lines bound together by metal rings. In the metal rings was a sharpened yellow pencil. I reached forward to touch it but Marvin pulled it from my grip, his eyes narrowed. I half expected a territorial snarl.

"Where did you get that?" I asked.

"There's special shops," he said, opening the book to a page that had faded pencil scrawlings over it.

I was bewildered, not so much by the artefact itself but why a man so respected in his field as Marvin Clarke would own one. Over the years I've met many others like Marvin who feel a particular affinity towards antiquated practices, creating false memories of inanimate objects with a longing to be associated with a more appealing era. These kinds of people sneer at those who do not hold a similar interest in the preservation of history, yet fail to give a reason as to why any of it still matters. Perhaps gripping onto ideals makes them feel as though they are more, as if having a time-consuming habit or obsession is akin to a religion or a political stance.

Rather than seeming cultured or wealthy with his paper book, Marvin appeared childlike. He didn't know why he had that thing but he had it and I didn't. That was enough for him.

As if in comical comparison, Lane rammed the tiny, battered memory card that held their entire report into the slot on the side of the table. After a few seconds, David's patient number was projected onto the white wall opposite us, quickly followed by the photo that had been taken of him when he was first admitted. With his eyes half-closed and his matted hair in clumps and tufts he looked like a day-old corpse.

"David Myre, VDA case," Marvin said, hacking up a throaty cough. "Twenty-eight-year-old white male, roughly six feet tall, no confirmation of his weight at the time of starting this report. Dark brown eyes, medium brown hair dyed black, size eleven feet. No piercings, tattoos or distinguishing scars..."

Over the next hour, Marvin relayed information about David's appearance, family background, academic achievements and working history in an unhurried fashion while Lane clicked through accompanying slides. There was also footage of classmates, colleagues and a few distant relatives answering simple questions in a matter-of-fact way about David's life. It was a long and arduous process, particularly as David had such an uninteresting existence.

It turned out that most of David's relatives had been well educated with jobs classified at grade three and above but, with the exception of his parents (who were comparably underachievers), David hadn't had regular contact with anyone in his family. Perhaps as a result, David was a middling to below average student who didn't appear to take academia too seriously, an attitude his peers verified when interviewed. Those who were close to him described him as oversensitive and those who weren't labelled him shy. He left education as a young teenager with few qualifications and even fewer acquaintances, proceeding to take up a basic employment in a garment factory where he frequently requested work in differing departments every few months. Aside from his apparent restlessness he was healthy and consistent – until his mid-twenties, that is.

Lane clicked through to a photograph showing warning letters addressed to David from his employers. Marvin stared unblinking at them as he spoke: "He stopped going to work at twenty-four and gave excuses to begin with, mostly saying he had diarrhoea or sickness or headaches. Stuff like that. It went on for so long there was an investigation, and when they checked his pass for his apartment building they found he went out nearly every day, but not to work. They thought he had another job to get double pay, so he was sent these warning letters. Loads of doctor appointments were made for him as well but he never showed up to them. A doctor called at his apartment five times to look at him but he was never there.

"He received a few fines and minor black marks on his employment record, but because he didn't sign up for government aid I don't think anyone paid too much attention to him."

Lane showed David's attendance record for the factory, which descended from abysmal to non-existent. Usually there would have been at least a short prison term for such a prolonged absence, but there must have been more pressing issues with the records office at the time; although his wages were eventually stopped, David remained an official employee with the factory up until his admittance to Boar House.

“Where did he go when he wasn’t at his apartment? Did you find out?”

Marvin scoffed. Of course he had found out.

“It’s a bit strange. For a while he kept going to a property two miles away, owned by Eric and Cynthia Harmon. They lived there with their son, Daniel, and their older daughter, Valerie, who had been in the same class as David at school. Valerie gave David a set of keys to the place and he’d go there while the Harmons were at work – or at school, in Daniel’s case.”

“What was he doing there?”

“Only Valerie knew he’d been there, the rest of the family hadn’t a clue until I told them during the interview, but Valerie said she never found out what he actually did. He had just asked to hang out at the house as a favour. After six months she said he scuffed a wall with his shoes or some shit like that and took the keys off him.”

“Why didn’t she ask what he wanted the house for? And why didn’t she want her parents to know about it?”

“No idea. We couldn’t get anything out of her. Legally she didn’t have to talk to us about it.”

“So where did he go after that?”

“Well, then it got a bit weirder,” Marvin said, the amusement evident in his voice. “When he wasn’t allowed at the Harmons’ anymore he just stopped leaving his apartment. He was holed up in there for almost three and a half years. He never left. Not once. Not until he was admitted here."

"So let me get this straight, he stopped going to work to hang out at the Harmons' house for six months and then hid in his apartment for three and a half years? Are you completely sure of that?"

Marvin glared at me. Of course he was sure.

"Did he have any visitors?"

"Psychiatrists did some home visits during his application for Boar House. There was also Trent Williams. He went round every now and then."

"Who is he? Do you know anything about him?"

"Trent? No spouse or kids. Forty-two. He's lived all over with his job, installing air conditioning units, and moved into the apartment building opposite David, around about two months after David became a hermit. Trent said they met when he did a job for him and they became friends. He has no criminal record or any reports of unusual activity, except… well, he has a bit of a grim pastime."

Lane projected copies of visitation requests from relief facilities all over the country onto the wall, each with the exact same signature on the dotted line. From what I could tell with a cursory glance there was a wide variety of patients; men, women, young, old, all with different reasons for relief.

"What is this?"

"That first visitation request was for Trent to visit his uncle dying of throat cancer in Birmingham. In the last ten years he's visited nine people. We don't know much about the others, except they're not relatives of his and he visited them only once. We weren't allowed to see their records or get any transcripts, but seeing as he's coming in soon we thought you might want to ask him about it."

The skin on the back of my neck began to tingle. I made a few notes to distract myself, to pretend there was some order to my thoughts.

"Okay, moving on," I said, looking back up again. "Where did David get his money if he wasn't working and didn't sign up for government aid?"

"He chipped into the savings he inherited from his grandparents. When that ran out his parents wired him money every month."

"So they were his anonymous benefactors?"

"Yup."

Even David's withdrawal from society was infuriatingly unclear. I stared at the hairs splaying out of Marvin's nostrils as he waded through facts and figures, my nails digging into my legs as I felt myself losing grip of the case.

After viewing David's bank statements, Lane clicked through to three headshot photographs of women, all middle-aged, white and brunette. "We chased the reports from the psychiatrists he saw before being admitted to Boar House," Marvin said. "These are the ones who were most involved in his case. The first one is a community doctor, the second a psychiatrist and relief specialist, and the third is his final psychotherapist."

I waited for him to continue while studying the bland, bodiless faces floating on the wall. When it was clear he wasn't going to add anything else, I was forced to prompt him. "That's it? All patients have to see at least four separate specialists. Is it even legal for one person to act as both a psychiatrist and relief specialist?"

Marvin exhaled loudly. "I've worked thousands more cases than you'll ever see, so I know what's normal and what's not, which is why I chased it up half a dozen times. I was so up the arses of the people at the records office, that by the end of it I could see out their nose holes, but these are definitely the only people who worked with David. Whether it was a special request or not I don't know, no one seemed to know, it was just done this way."

"So someone requested for him to only see these three people?"

Marvin shrugged. "I said I don't know. If that happened it wasn't on file and it wasn't spoken about in their clinics. Some of their reports weren't even written at the time we asked for them, so we had to wait for them to be finished."

Incompetence? Or intentional?

"Do the reports say much?"

"Not really. Just that he seemed depressed and tired, reclusive. That sort of thing."

Lane clicked through a few pages of therapy reports that had clearly been written to the standard guidelines but had not been embellished in any way.

By the time we came to the last section of the WORM report, the search through his apartment and belongings, I'd had enough of the never-ending obstructions.

"We found nothing," Marvin said.

I snorted. "You've been telling me nothing in great detail for some time now."

Marvin leant forward, a sneer on his cracked lips. "No, we actually found nothing."

"What do you mean?"

"We arrived at the site at twelve fifteen. The keyhole to the front door had never been used, as there were no scratch marks on the surface where it would have received the key. The door handle was new and it had been cleaned with domestic polish. I detected fibres from a dusting cloth. The door itself was freshly painted, the tests indicate around three weeks before. The doormat was brand new with only small traces of dust that I think came from..."

"Please don't tell me I have to listen to a chemical dissection of the entire apartment before you tell me there's nothing to gleam from any of this. Get to the point, if there is one."

Marvin glanced at his wife, his jaw tightening. She didn't look at him but began to wring her hands in mirrored aggravation.

Marvin indicated for me to look at the projection. There were photographs of what I assumed to be David's apartment; plain cream walls, white painted shelves, a cream carpet, a spotless white oven, a bare grey mattress and a toilet with a plastic sticker on the lid.

"All of the furniture and fittings are new," Marvin said, "and it's all been painted and cleaned as well. There's loads of calcium hypochlorite all over the surfaces but also loads of high grade chemicals everywhere, a lot of them VOCs so the place must have been vacant for a while unless David had some sort of gas mask on the whole time. Just in case you were wondering, a VOC is a volatile organic compound, it means..."

"I know what the acronym stands for," I said.

"Acronym?"

I sighed. "All right," I said, raising my hand, "so there was...nothing."

Marvin nodded. "Literally nothing. Not one single thing, not even a hair."

"What about content? What stuff did he leave?"

"Sheets and towels, all new and washed within an inch of their lives, cutlery and plates all standard issue from the past few months, some still with their approval stickers on and stacked in the cupboards. There was a bottle of unopened water in the fridge, still in date... that's it."

Marvin was enjoying my suffering and took no care to hide it.

"So what the hell does this mean?" I asked. "He never really lived there? It's some sort of stage apartment?"

"No. He definitely lived there, we have evidence from CCTV and witness reports."

"So how is the apartment like this?"

Thoughts of David having OCD were quickly quashed when I thought of his yellow teeth, his long nails with grit underneath, his poorly dyed hair and its uneven cut, his stained, tatty clothes in the belongings locker…

No, he definitely didn't have OCD.

"He used cleaners," Marvin said. I looked up at the projection, which showed a photograph of three men with shaved heads leaving David's apartment building. The next photograph showed them clambering into a van with a logo on the side that read Grays Hill Cleaning Company.

I looked at the two WORMs, my thoughts no longer processing into words. Suddenly Lane's face was inches from mine, her musty breath blowing flyaway hairs from my face. "They cleaned the place for three solid days a week before he was admitted here," she said, her voice crackling with underuse, "all paid for by his parents. We found out as much as we could in the time we had, but with all the delays to this case we couldn't find out much more."

I knew what that meant. It meant they couldn't do anything else, so I had to go to the apartment. I had to speak with his parents. I had to find the rest out on my own.

"He's hiding something," she said.

"Really?" Marvin said, scraping his chair back and standing up to leave. "Oh, my dear, where would we be without your valuable insight?"

# 8

I had hoped Logue would remain absent for the majority of the case, but at the next assessment he succeeded once again in disappointing me.

"How lovely of you to show," I said.

Logue lowered himself into the chair beside me. I thought of the last time I saw him and the unreserved anger spewing from his mouth. Now he just looked fragile and empty.

"I got the WORM report," I told him, more out of professional courtesy than anything.

Logue nodded, busying himself with the bag on his lap. "I read it."

"Thoughts?"

"None in particular."

"I wish I could say that surprised me."

He let out a short, sharp exhale through his nose. "What do you want me to say? It's not going to affect the case much. WORM reports never do. Anyway, there's nothing in it."

"Too much nothing. And too much nothing is something."

"What does that even mean?"

"Are you honestly saying you don't think he's trying to hide something?"

Logue placed his e-Noter and texter carefully onto the table before turning to face me. His watery eyes were bordered with prominent blood vessels and his thin top lip curled inward as he spoke. "Everyone has secrets."

"How insightful."

"Nothing major can be hidden from the WORMs, you've seen what they can do. If there was something to be found they would have found it. The report is nothing but conjecture."

"Thanks, Logue, I'll be sure to take your incredibly wise words on board." I enjoyed watching his jaw click left and right as I provoked him. "Did you even read the section about the cleaners?"

"Yes."

"And?"

I could see it almost caused him physical pain to respond. "It doesn't mean anything."

"It means everything, don't you see? What was he trying to cover up?"

"If he's trying to hide something it's probably something embarrassing and inconsequential, like a porn habit or a petty crime, or something he thinks matters but in reality no one gives a shit. It happens all the time. Or maybe he trashed the apartment so hired cleaners to get the deposit back, who the hell knows? All the information we need on him is accounted for, and the cleaners wouldn't hush up anything serious– why would they? You need to stop speculating and just concentrate on the evidence."

"What do you have to say about the Harmons, then?"

"He wanted somewhere to go that wasn't his apartment, probably to alleviate feelings of guilt for slacking off from work. I've seen that kind of thing before. You've got to realise how hard it is for people of that employment grade, they can't get anywhere in life, not really. They either work hard for no reward or are made to feel like leaches. He was taking money from his parents so he clearly felt conflicted about the whole thing. He needed an escape."

"You seem to have all the answers. And the visitation request? Why is he being visited by a man who has seen more VDA patients than I have? You just can't dismiss that."

"I don't know, maybe he likes helping people out. Does it matter?"

Logue was refusing to bite, as if disregarding the facts would eventually make them disappear so he could carry on ignoring the world again. He was like a device running out of batteries, every now and again there was a surge of power and I would see the glimmer of the professional he might have once been, but a second later he would be on the verge of completely shutting down and was straight back into the queue for retirement.

"Well, if that's all you have to say, I suppose I'll update you on this morning's assessment," I said, opening David's file on my e-Noter. "I've decided to use the Eberhardt technique, so as you know it'll provide better results if only I talk. Just be as silent and unresponsive as usual and we might just get somewhere today."

He shook off my remark. "Is it wise to use the Eberhardt? He's not uncooperative. He does talk."

"He avoids, and we haven't got time for that. He needs to start relenting control if he's to benefit from his time here."

Logue's jaw tightened again momentarily but his voice was slow and calm. "Will it not antagonise him? He's the type to resist the Eberhardt."

"I think I can handle it."

And just like that he conceded, giving a half-shrug as his face became devoid of expression. I was really starting to hate the way he regarded every conversation with me as an errand to be put off until later.

A few minutes later, David was brought into the room by his phys aid. Despite upping his nutritional intake and intensifying the physiotherapy sessions he still required support while walking, but there was a definite steadiness to his step and a pinkness to his complexion that hadn't been there before.

Once helped to his chair, David fought against his naturally hunched posture to sit up as straight as he was able. I suspected he wasn't about to make the session easy for me – there was hostility in the way he held himself.

I began with a neutral question: "How have things been since the last time we spoke?"

"Tolerable."

From that I immediately knew the Eberhardt was the correct choice. There was a facade with him that had to be broken down if we were to gain any useable evidence for the committee. Or for my desistance theory.

"In this session I'm just going to be asking some questions," I said, careful not to use any terms or phrases that could affect the technique. "They might seem a bit strange or unconnected, but if you could just answer them as quickly and as honestly as you can it shouldn't take too long. Is that okay?"

"Yup," he replied, folding his arms neatly.

I had no written questions for the session. The Eberhardt commanded an impulsiveness and rapidness that prepared notes would hinder.

I began with the most recent findings. "Do you know what a WORM report is?"

"Nope."

"That's the search you agreed to when you were admitted. The WORMs are external investigators who work outside of the facility."

"Ah yes, them. They looked through my things."

As dictated by the technique, I kept my voice low and stern. "We found your apartment quite interesting, can you think why that might be?"

"Nope."

There was something conflicted about his expression, perhaps an uncertainty that he was trying to quash with nonchalance.

"It was clean, very clean. Did someone help you with that?"

"I cleaned it before I left. The landlady asked me to."

"So you're saying you cleaned the apartment entirely by yourself?"

"I said so, didn't I?"

"What did you use to clean it?"

"I don't know, bleach probably."

I expected to see some sort of excitement or realisation reflecting in Logue's eyes but there was nothing. I could now prove David was lying to us, but Logue was unreachable wherever he was, lost in his own unimportance.

I forced myself to put my focus back on David. The Eberhardt technique dictated that no more than five questions should be asked on any particular subject. As I had now reached my limit for discussing his apartment, it was time to move on.

"Do you have any friends?"

His first instinct was to laugh, but then he paused to really consider the question. As I needed his responses to be immediate, I quickly followed it up with: "Are you close with anyone, perhaps neighbours or colleagues?"

His hands, which had been folded across his chest, now moved to settle over his groin. I made a note that he had begun to display signs of self-protection.

"Not really."

"Please clarify."

"I've said 'hi' to some people when they've said 'hi' to me, that sort of thing."

His voice was quieter and at a lower pitch. I made a note about isolation.

"Do you speak to your family?"

"Nope."

"Why not?"

"Now that's a complicated question. Don't all families have a black sheep? You'd have to ask them about it."

"Yes, I plan to."

I thought I detected a momentary widening of the eyes, but I could have been mistaken. I was never very proficient at reading micro-expressions.

"To save you the trouble," he said, "we're just different. No animosity, no feuds, no great showdown. And there's no need to bother them about it. I just like to be by myself."

I made a note to prioritise the investigation of the parents.

"What do you like to do by yourself?"

He laughed. "I'm a man, what do you think I like to do?"

Using sexual connotations was a cheap ploy to embarrass me and dismiss the subject of his family. I knew exactly what subject to counteract his remark with.

"When was the last time you had sexual intercourse?"

The expulsion of laughter, followed by a glance in Logue's direction, revealed an intense level of discomfort for the question that I hadn't anticipated. I made a note about it.

"It doesn't need to be specific," I said, "you can just give me the month, or even the year." He smiled at that. "Do you remember the last time?"

There were another few seconds of silence. As I was about to ask another question he stopped me with a raised hand and said, "Have you *ever* had sex? Like, has anyone actually wanted to fuck you?"

I'm hesitant to admit it, but he caught me off guard. Even with his palpable uneasiness he managed to push against my questioning. There was a lack of shame in him and an overpowering confidence that didn't fit at all with the profile of a male VDA patient.

"This isn't about me," I said, sounding more agitated than I had intended. "How regularly on average do you have sex?"

His arms dropped to his sides. His formerly stiff legs relaxed, and splayed sideward in a calm and open position. He no longer felt the need to guard himself.

I began to panic.

"David, how many partners have you..."

He held up his hand again to cut me off. “I don’t really see how these questions are helpful to you. You’re clearly trying to humiliate me, but it won’t work. If you want to ask me how I am, why I’m doing this or what I discussed with my other therapists, then go ahead. I’m here to die and it’s my right to do that, I don’t need this shit.”

He was now setting down boundaries, forcibly pushing me into a direction he was more comfortable with. I had to push back.

“Do you fail to perform?”

He smirked and leaned back, interlocking his fingers behind his head. “I don’t know, but I probably would with you.”

I gave in to irritation at this point.

“Will you not answer me because there’s nothing to say about your sex life?” His smirk widened into a broad grin, the grey creased skin bunching up in the corners of his mouth. “Or maybe you’re sexually perverted? Is that why you’re unwilling to talk about it? Do you fantasize about the wrong things? The wrong people? Perhaps you’ve thought of your parents sexually? Is that why you don’t talk to them anymore?”

Logue leapt out of his seat, which startled both David and I. “I think we need to stop this now.”

I also stood, staring disbelieving at Logue while he struggled to look me in the eye.

He cleared his throat. “The patient is clearly being subjected to...”

“Outside,” I snapped, the heat of my anger swelling beneath my skin as I walked towards the door. I heard David snort as Logue followed me in a meek, compliant shuffle.

In the corridor, Logue's assertiveness well and truly evaporated and he became flat and morose, his head hung like a chastised dog. Without thinking, I pushed him into an empty room across the hall. The loud clatter of the door as it slammed shut behind me was immensely satisfying.

"Are you willing to jeopardise everything, this entire case and both of our careers, just because you can't stomach a difficult assessment?" I asked, trying to contain my anger. "Do you know what you're doing? What you've just done?"

A glimmer of certainty returned in him. "You're embarrassing yourself. You're supposed to be asking him things that could help with the case, not barraging him with sick accusations."

"If you had a degree of foresight, you would know I'm working to get the results we need to clean up the catastrophic mess you've made."

"What results? What have we actually got from this?"

"That he has some deep-seeded issues when it comes to relationships. His relationships and sex life are now significant factors for his treatment."

"There's no way you can claim that, you're just trying to justify the inappropriate things you've said to him."

"I know this technique might be a little modern for you, but it has been certified by the committee and is commonly used nowadays."

"So other euthanasists regularly accuse their patients of incest?"

"I didn't accuse, I suggested. It's part of the technique to break down his defences."

Logue sat heavily on a bare patient bed. "This is what's wrong here. With all of you. You just want the job finished, no matter what it takes, but these are desperate, pained people, you can't force them into a confession. They're not criminals. The man in there is thinking he wants to die, and all you want to do is torture a reaction out of him so the committee has something to agree on. We're here to help him find relief, not push him over the edge to get the result we want."

"So you're suggesting we make everything as stress-free and painless as possible? We'll help him drift through the process, ease him into dying nice and gently because we couldn't possibly ask him any awkward questions, could we? If he fails at committee that's not our problem, at least he wasn't put under any undue stress. He's *lying* to us, Logue, and he's trying to cover it up. We can't do anything to help him until we find out the truth, can't you see that?"

Logue shook his head. "You are being absolutely ridiculous."

"It's our job to treat patients, no matter how uncomfortable it makes us feel. No matter what's said by the patient's family, protesters or even Watts. Death is unattractive and gruesome, but it is what it is and I can't understand why you're struggling with it after all these years. If we need to push patients over the edge to be sure we're doing the right thing then at least we're doing it in a safe environment so they can be protected."

A romanticised view of death is a psychological contagion for a euthanasist. Logue's fictional interpretation of relief was not only difficult to watch, but would eventually cause more suffering than it prevented. He had to be contained and isolated from the weak and vulnerable. He had to be kept away from David.

I opened the door, ready for the conversation to be over, but Logue stood to continue his feeble argument.

"We're not selling death," he said. "We're here to help people."

"Maybe you don't mind failing your patients, Logue, but I do. I want to do what that man in there wants, what he came to us for. He wants relief, and for him that means the relief procedure. Do you think he wants the alternative? To be sent to a mental institution until he dies of old age? Times have changed – we don't need to keep apologising for our work anymore, we're providing patients with a medical service and we need to fulfil our duties to them."

"Then why are you humiliating him?"

"Because I need to be certain that what he wants is worth putting his life and my career on the line for. I need to give the committee irrefutable evidence. I need to do my job."

"You're looking at this all backwards."

I shrugged. "Well maybe that's the way we're supposed to be looking at it. You're the only one challenging my methods."

"Sanity is not statistical."

Logue was breathing heavily and trembling and I could see nothing left of him to argue with. I left before he could say another word, determined to pick up the momentum of the Eberhardt technique with David and conclude the assessment before the allotted time ran out. No more wasted chances.

I strode back across the corridor and typed in the security code into the panel on the wall. As I pulled back the door my body tensed instinctively. Something didn't feel right.

As I stepped in, everything in the room was where it had been, the desk and the equipment all laid out as before, all except the chair David had been sitting on. It was on its side. I began to edge out backwards and collided roughly with Logue.

"What's going on?" he asked, trying to peer over my shoulder.

"I can't believe we did that," I said, looking up and down the corridor. "Why the hell did we leave him on his own?"

"What's happened?"

"I can't believe it."

"What?"

"He's gone. David's not in there."

# 9

Logue pushed me aside to see for himself. "Maybe a psych aid took him back to his room?"

"Don't be stupid. They know I'd crucify them if they moved him without my permission."

"But how did he open the door?"

"He can't be far. He's so weak, he can't walk five seconds without clinging to the walls."

"How did he get out?"

I looked left and right, trying to work out which way he was more inclined to go. To the right were unlocked double doors that led to the fire escape stairwell, but they were incredibly heavy – probably too heavy for David to have opened, and in any case they made a loud thud when swinging to a close. I would definitely have heard that from across the hall. There were also security guards posted on each floor who would have notified me immediately upon David's detainment.

To the left was a long corridor split into shorter sections by security doors, all requiring a five-digit code to open, but David could have memorised that when the phys aid had brought him through. I doubt many members of staff adhered to protocol by covering the panel with their hand while typing in the code, especially if they were simultaneously propping up an emaciated and incredibly unsteady six-foot tall man.

Aside from the staff dealing with patients in the surrounding rooms, there wouldn't have been many people around at that time of day. If I acted fast, there was still a chance of finding him before anyone else did.

As I turned to the left, Logue grabbed my shoulder and hauled me back, slamming me hard against the wall.

"Jesus!"

"Where the hell are you going?" Logue said, his face far too close to mine.

I could feel my back already beginning to swell from impacting against the edge of the doorframe. "I'm going to find him."

"We need to tell security."

"I can find him, they don't need to know."

Logue's lip began to quiver and I felt a grotesque and intense desire to see him cry, but the quiver merely made way to a grimace.

"You're always talking about regulations," he said, nostrils flaring with each breath, "but what if he does something to himself? What if someone outside gets wind of this? We need to get security *now*."

I pushed him away from me, despising the heat of his body transferring to mine.

"Stop panicking. Ten minutes, that's all I need. If you search the fire escape and I search the corridor we're bound to find him. If we can't manage to find a half-starved patient in ten minutes I'm more than happy for you to call security, but just hold off for now. We don't want to make this more dramatic than it needs to be."

Logue began to shake his head, but I could tell he was about to agree.

"Ten minutes," he said, kicking the wall beside me and heading off to the right.

I made my way down the corridor but didn't run, acutely aware of what could happen if I drew attention to myself. No one needed to find out, and in any case David had limited freedom; the code he had seen the phys aid use only worked for three security doors, and from there the corridor split in differing directions. Even if he somehow got through all that he would still have to contend with Boar House's maze of endless lino and windowless walls.

I began by searching the nearby rooms. Most of them held assessments and were empty save a table and chairs, but others housed trolleys, piles of laundry and broken equipment. I couldn't imagine finding David hiding in a corner, peering guiltily from behind a wonky IV stand, but I searched them all anyway. I was convinced there was some sort of purpose to his escape or at least a destination in mind.

After the first security door, all of the rooms in that section were occupied by patients, the majority of which were elderly and comatose. Some were skeletal and sunken, as if their beds were consuming them, their slow moving eyes following me and their slack mouths uttering indecipherable pleas while I checked beneath their beds for any sign of David.

There was a small group of visitors bustling around the room at the end of the corridor. I tried to push my way through but a hand on my shoulder prevented me from getting past. I turned to see a woman, formally dressed in a navy suit with short, slick hair, pointing to the patient surrounded by visitors. “I’m sorry,” she said in a tone so insincerely apologetic I wasn’t sure whether she was mocking me or not, “do you mind coming in to see my father? He’s been asking for something to help him sleep.”

In seven minutes Logue would call security. Probably sooner if he was panicking.

“Please,” she said, sensing I was about to refuse. “He hasn’t slept in three days and no one’s come by the room in a really long time.”

Sighing, I moved her aside to get into the room. The air was damp and smelled like fresh disinfectant and stale urine. The patient, an old man breathing heavily, had an audience of middle-aged men and women, all in various states of discomfort and restlessness.

I pulled his chart to one side and scanned it for an overview of his condition. The patient was terminally ill with bowel cancer, and on the highest possible dose of morphine as well as a myriad of other medications. There was no way he could be given anything else – I was surprised he wasn’t unconscious already.

“Just let me sleep, please,” he rasped. “I just want to go to sleep now.”

His daughter nodded encouragingly to me, as if his moans were confirmation of his diagnosis.

I began backing away towards the door, realising my exit would have to be swift. “I’m afraid I won’t be able to prescribe him anything,” I said. “He looks stable at the moment, but he...”

The daughter grinned and gave a thumbs up to the rest of the visitors. “Stable! I told you lot we should have waited!” She turned back to me.”His relief is in two days, now he’s stable how do we go about stopping it? Do we take him off some of his medication so that we can get him some sleeping tablets or something? Can we move him back to the hospital? What can we do?"

Saliva ran from the man's open mouth as he began to sob. "I want to sleep," he whispered, dribbling with each syllable, the pain and exhaustion ridding him of any concern for composure. I wanted to pull the pillow from beneath his head and press it firmly onto his miserable face; his family had forced him to live for long enough.

But it was out of my hands. All I could do was shake my head and back further from the room. "He's stable but still very unwell. It doesn't mean he's necessarily going to get better, he's just not getting any worse right now. There's not much more I can do for him, but if you want to pause his relief your best option would be to speak to his euthanasist and ask for their advice."

Before the daughter could respond I hurried from the room, a joyous feeling of ease flooding the entirety of my body as the security door clicked shut and locked behind me.

After searching another four or five rooms with no sign of David, I really began to doubt myself. If he had managed to leave the premises I would be imprisoned for negligence, or at the very least forced to leave Boar House indefinitely. I would have to register as homeless and camp near a shelter until I was permitted a room, which could take months. After that it was a matter of luck and desperation. I momentarily toyed with the idea of becoming an apprentice sweep, but the facility wouldn't allow me back onto the premises. The industry would be completely closed to me.

No, I could never go back. I would most likely be pushed into menial work and, for my own safety, would have to spend the rest of my life hiding my former profession from co-workers, neighbours and anyone else I happened to meet. Disgraced euthanasists were seen as fair game.

As I wondered aimlessly from room to room, my desperation intensifying, I saw a clump of dark hair bowed down on the far side of a patient's bed. I tasted coppery blood as my teeth pierced the tip of my tongue.

David was engrossed in the face of a frail, blue-tinged woman. Her skin somehow seemed both tightly stretched and loose, all held in place by a yellowing, spotted scalp. She was unconscious, yet David was muttering to her, his hand close but not quite touching hers. I stood in front of the doorway and gripped onto the frame, readying myself for confrontation.

"What are you doing in here?" I asked. I had meant for a level of detachment but the words that fell out of my mouth were more of a staunch accusation. Despite the harshness of my tone he didn't react.

Just as I was deciding my next move, he said, "I've just been looking around,"

In the quiet that followed, all I could hear were David's laboured breaths. I then felt a retch of panic as I realised the machines attached to the patient were not making their habitual rhythmic bleeps. Fear of what I might have found froze me to the floor, but I relented to logic and rushed for the monitor at the foot of the bed.

I drew back the screen and opened the stats. Her vitals were weak but there were no signs of distress. The alerts bar had merely been muted, perhaps to allow her to sleep.

"I haven't done anything to her if that's what you're thinking," he said.

His sincerity meant nothing. I selected the emergency check-up icon on the monitor – a phys aid would arrive within a few minutes.

"We need to get back," I said, moving forward to take hold of David's arm just above the elbow. He didn't resist, and was light enough to pull up onto his feet with one hand. "What are you even doing in here? You must have been told you can't travel alone anywhere in the facility."

As I stopped at the doorway to type a message to Logue, David's breathing became a staggered gulp followed by sharp propulsions of air from his mouth. Worried he may be close to a hyperventilating, I simply sent the words 'Got him' to Logue, lifted David's arm over my shoulders and began to drag him down the corridor. It seemed that outside the confines of the assessment room his calm, controlled manner had broken down into fits of anxiety.

"I was just..." he began, stumbling over his own feet. There was another sharp intake of breath before he could speak again. "I was just seeing what it looked like."

"What do you mean?"

"Dying. I wanted to see what dying looked like."

I suppressed the urge to sink my nails into his forearm. "I'm not sure I follow."

"I've never seen anyone die. I've never seen a corpse."

"You're worrying about things that are of no concern to you at the moment. You need to take your treatment a day at a time, and for now that means putting on weight and being honest with us."

"Don't you think it's strange?" His throat rasped as he tried to compete with the loud buzz of the unlocking security door. "Most people never see death or dying their whole lives even…even though it's normal. It's hidden away. It's not right…to live like we do, it's not good."

It was usually only the terminally ill patients who believed their morbid musings were particularly poignant. Such talk was tiresome and never the profound, unique philosophies the orator believed they were expressing.

"The patient you disturbed is going through her own pain right now," I said. "She doesn't need you staring at her just so you can satisfy your sudden fascination with death."

His shoulders stiffened. "But I didn't do anything, I doubt she even noticed I was there."

David's strides lengthened and his breathiness eased.

"Where are we going?" he asked.

"Back to the assessment room."

"Can't I just go back to my room? I'm tired."

"We still have some time left," I said, trying to peer down at the fob watch, "I think we have another fifteen minutes."

I was also exhausted, but I couldn't allow the Eberhardt technique to finish incorrectly. It had to be on my terms if we were to get anywhere with the pacing of David's relief.

"Where's that other doctor? Will he be in there?"

I doubted it. "Mr Logue is a euthanasist, not a doctor. Anyway we're here now."

As predicted, the assessment room was empty and I was forced to half-carry, half-drag David in unassisted. I knew I wasn't strong enough to lower his lanky body onto the chair by myself so I had no choice but to drop him onto it. I brought him as close to the seat as possible but he still thudded hard onto the plastic frame, wincing and sucking in his teeth upon impact, hands clawing at his thighs until the pain from the sores subsided. His lips were pale and there was a shimmer of sweat coating his forehead, but it couldn't have been helped.

In any case, I felt it to be a fair punishment.

I sat opposite, a tremble in my fingers beginning to trickle up my arms. It was too early in the case for so many mistakes to have been made yet it was far too late to correct them all. The only thing I could do was build upon the broken foundations already formed.

David began to hyperventilate again. "Breathe slowly, in through the nose and out through the mouth" I said. His eyes bulged as he struggled to inhale. "You know I'm trying to help you, don't you?"

He nodded.

"Then why are you making this so hard for yourself? Why did you leave the room?"

He closed his eyes and thought for a moment, the process of which seemed to calm him a little. "I felt trapped."

"What do you mean? You're not a prisoner here, you voluntarily admitted yourself. You can request to leave whenever you want."

He'd be immediately institutionalised, but he was still free to leave.

"I know that. It just feels so claustrophobic here."

"I don't understand. You hadn't left your apartment for years before coming here. You went through a lot to get to this point, have you changed your mind about relief?"

"Yes…I mean no, no I haven't. I haven't changed my mind. I can't change my mind. The thing is, I used to be able to forget about things for a while. At the apartment I was alone but I could forget about myself. Here I can't control what I think and talk about. It's all about me all the time. Earlier you were asking me about things that meant nothing, more than nothing, so I just had to get out to remind myself why I'm doing this. I needed to remember what's real." He paused to catch his breath. "I need to be here, but going through it over and over is... agony. I want it to stop, but it's just going on and on and on. I don't know, I just want to tear a hole in the world and escape."

At that point I *knew*. I knew where others had failed him, where Logue had failed him, I had the ability to succeed. With time I would be able to diagnose him as desistant or curable and relieve him of this indecision. He would be able to accept treatment without doubt in his mind. He should never have had to face that quandary – if a patient with cancer isn't forced to make decisions about their wellbeing, why should his relief be any different?

I had so much work to do with him, but the session had reached a natural conclusion. I didn't want to taint that.

"Okay, I think that's enough for today," I said, closing the session with my texter. As the cameras and microphones whirred and died I sent an alert for a phys aid to take David back to his room.

"So," I said, feeling an unusual compulsion to relieve the tension in the room, "how exactly did you get out of here earlier?"

He shrugged. "I got up and stopped the door with my foot before it closed."

The disappointment of the truth ended any desire I had to converse further.

I stood and began packing up my things to leave. As I bent forward to pick up my e-Noter, David grabbed my wrist with surprising strength.

"I've got to know," he said, already beginning to shake with the effort of holding me so tightly, "have you ever thought about it?"

His jagged fingernails were digging into my skin, but I managed to pull myself free from his grip. "Thought about what?"

"Suicide."

One step forward, three steps back. "You're not in the process of suicide, David. Do you mean have I ever considered applying for relief?" He nodded. "I believe every citizen has the right to relief. Our bodies are our own, and just as we have the right to be treated for mental and physical illnesses we have the right to..."

"I don't want that bullshit," he said. "You've turned the cameras off, the session is over, you can say what you want now. So? Have you ever thought about it?"

"Yes, of course I have. If I found out I was terminally ill there would be no question of whether I'd do it. Definitely."

"But have you ever just thought about it? Just ending it? Just stopping everything?"

I hesitated. "If I needed to."

"But what if you didn't need to? What if you wanted to?"

"Maybe, if I felt that way."

He sighed. "You don't get it."

"I do. This is a difficult process and you want to feel as though you're doing the right thing. You want me to reassure you, to give you validation, but I can't right now. We'll work it out together, it's just going to take some time."

"But I've seen the way you look at me. You think I'm weak. You pity me so much you're frightened of me."

"What? I'm not frightened of you, David."

I knew I hadn't sounded very convincing, but the words had been said and I couldn't think of a way to take them back.

# 10

The protective shield covering the windows gave everything a grey hue, and the dirty flecks and streaks over its plastic created odd shadows that floated like seaweed across the room. Watts saw me looking and scowled.

"This is nothing too formal," he said, straightening the handful of objects that decorated his desk, "I just want to be kept up to speed."

I nodded. "Of course, Dr Watts."

"Call me Lucas, please."

I felt my eyebrows rise involuntarily. How would he react if were I to take that comment seriously?

He leant forward on the desk, a faint smile on his lips. "So what's new?"

"Well, I've carried out a few basic assessments," I said, looking to my notes, "I received the WORM report and I've been readying things for the physical examination. What's interesting is…"

"We'll get to all that in a minute. First, tell me what happened."

"What happened?"

"A little bird told me you had an escapee."

A cold judder ran through me, a sensation not too dissimilar to the aftermath of an intense bout of vomiting. Perhaps Watts' smile was supposed to be warm and sympathetic, as if to apologise for the vulgarity of the confrontation, but it felt more like an attempt to disguise his immense satisfaction.

"I'm not sure what you mean," I said.

"Don't do that. Don't act clueless when you're anything but, Nieve. It's an insult to you as much as it is to me. I'm talking about your VDA patient. Something Myre... Is it Daniel?"

"David."

It didn't matter that he knew, it mattered *how* he knew. I was relatively confident that no one had seen David leave the assessment room, so unless Logue had mentioned something in a fit of panic it was likely I was being watched.

Watts was trying to hide his grin like a child getting their sibling in trouble. "Don't look so petrified, Nieve. Myre mentioned it to his psych aid, probably assuming he already knew, and the psych aid reported it to me. Of course I said I would investigate it, but I'm sure you have a perfectly reasonable explanation as to what happened."

Would David really have told his psych aid about it? Then again, Watts had no reason to go to the trouble of lying to me –head doctors always had plenty of other people to do their lying for them.

"What did David say?" I asked.

"All in good time. I'd like to know your side of it first, if you don't mind."

"Have you spoken to Logue about it yet?"

"No, I haven't spoken to him. Why, was he involved?"

"Yes." I had said it without thinking, but there was no going back on it now. I stared out into the murky plastic, which made the grounds below look smeared with fog. "I don't mean to speak out of turn here, it's not in my nature to…"

"Just spit it out, Nieve."

I cleared my throat. "He was in the room with me during the assessment. He sabotaged the Eberhardt technique and when I went to speak to him about it in the corridor he didn't close the door properly behind him. That's how David – the patient – managed to get out."

It felt a little distasteful at the time to say it, but I couldn't allow for Logue's past accomplishments to compensate for his recurring mistakes. The lingering remnants of respect Watts held for him were hindering rational thought, an error I had made once myself with a boy from my group home. I forget his name. I think I was nine or ten, and I never reported the boy's secret visits to his mother because he was shy and kind, and I hadn't understood why his family had been banned from visiting him. When the news broke out that the mother's boyfriend had repeatedly stamped on the boy's neck for thirty-two consecutive seconds until he stopped breathing, I knew I was to blame. Every child in that home who had seen him leave but remained silent had become a murderer. I will never make the same error of judgement again, especially as I can no longer blame the consequences on youthful ignorance.

Watts' smile had been replaced with exasperation. I understood his reluctance to retire euthanasists like Logue outright. It made more sense to phase him out rather than incite any unwanted attention, but the man was a liability. It was going to catch up with him soon enough.

Watts sighed heavily. "You've heard about what happened in Miller Park, I take it?"

I hadn't. I knew Miller Park was a larger relief centre located somewhere further north, but I didn't keep track of current affairs beyond the walls of Boar House. Nothing more than competitive stats and techniques anyway. Watts' tone implied that the incident was common knowledge, so all I could do was nod.

"Well, it's put me under a lot of pressure, and it's becoming difficult to keep Boar House as independent as it is at the moment. As it has been for many years. Everyone's on high alert and the government are beginning to crack down on every little problem they find, as you can well imagine, and the poor performance of Logue's department hasn't gone unnoticed. I didn't want the whole situation to get out of hand, so I accepted an ultimatum from the committee: either figures improve or we get rid of the department completely and accept outside assistance."

I knew what he meant by outside assistance. All non-standard cases would be sent to other facilities and our time would be taken up by internal investigations, reports, continual surveillance and undercover officials posing as patients. Boar House would have to pay for all of this out of its own pocket, meaning a heavy reduction in funding. Our reputation was strong but not strong enough to withstand that.

I had never experienced mental strain in a physical sense before, but at that point I could almost feel something dragging me down. Every word Watts said was another weight hanging and pulling down on my flesh.

"I'm going to be very honcst with you, Nieve." The way he said my name made me recoil slightly. "What you've told me about Bill is alarming. Ordinarily, I would impose an immediate sanction on him, but with all these eyes on us it's simply not possible to do so without creating severe problems for everyone within the facility. We'll put this to one side for now, and I'm going to ask you to do your best to distance Bill from your VDA case without causing suspicion. I fully appreciate the position I'm putting you in and I know it's a lot to ask, but it's all I can do right now. My hands are tied."

"So you want me to babysit him while solving the most challenging case of my career?"

"In a word, yes."

I tried to laugh but my body wouldn't allow it.

"Why don't you just tell him to back off yourself?"

"I've managed to put him on signed release a few times but there's only so long I can do that before people start to notice. I've also tried reducing his patients, but he's been holding onto the department for dear life."

Of course he had. What life did he have beyond his work? Why would he leave the only existence he had ever known and willingly submerge himself into the unknown?

Watts' phone began to ring, but he cancelled the call without so much as glancing at it. "I'm not going to deny that I've been struggling to come up with a solution to this. I've relied on Bill a lot in the past and he's helped god knows how many patients. Did you know that he drafted about twenty-five percent of our current patient protocols?"

I shook my head, knowing that if I spoke Watts would immediately sense my lack of interest.

"He was a visionary of sorts. Then again he's also the reason we had to introduce Article 17B."

My breath caught in my throat. “He was? Why? What happened?”

“He…well…” Watts swallowed, and it was the first and only time I have ever seen him look truly uncomfortable. “He started an inappropriate relationship with a patient’s wife.”

“And she moved into his cottage?”

He nodded, wiping fresh perspiration from his forehead with the back of his hand. “You see, technically they weren’t breaking any rules, which was why we had to introduce the article. If we had just banned patients and their relatives from living in the cottages, the press would have picked up on Logue immediately and we wouldn’t have survived the scrutiny. This way we could force her to leave along with all the staff’s partners and children and keep it all above board. No one suspected the real reason for it, they were too angered by the relocation of their families to notice. It was an incredibly turbulent time, as you can well imagine, but it needed to be done.

“Anyway, we’re not here to gossip. The main reason I wanted to talk to you today was because I think you represent the sort of direction I want Boar House to go in. You could really turn things around for the department and I want you to know you have my full support. Once this Miller Park nonsense is over with and things have calmed down, I can tell you’re going to do great things. We need a fresh outlook, and you have what it takes to make a difference.”

“But we would need to introduce prisoners to truly turn things around in the industry.”

I was waiting for irritation, but Watts just nodded. “Eventually, but you understand why we can’t consider that right now. We need to get through our current problems first."

"Yes, I understand."

"So you'll work with me on this?"

"I will do as much as I can to help."

"Wonderful. Now that's all dealt with, tell me about your progress with David."

The next half hour was spent discussing the case. Whenever I introduced a new topic Watts would request a briefer, more generalised overview, and if I dawdled on a matter for too long he would begin to tap his foot against the leg of his desk. I explained my interest in investigating Trent, the Harmons, the cleaners and David's relationship with his parents, but he dismissed it as nothing more than guesswork.

I concluded by requesting leave from the facility in order to interview David's parents and see his apartment for myself. Watts was initially reluctant but agreed to think about it, although he knew he would have no choice but to say yes eventually. I decided to pick the idea of interviewing the cleaners and the Harmons back up once I had proven to both him and myself that I was heading in the right direction.

Watts eventually made it clear that I had outstayed my welcome. We shook hands, his soft and cool fingers feeling slightly unreal against my rougher skin.

"If you need any assistance," he said, opening the door for me, "with *anything* to do with this case, don't hesitate to ask. We need this to be a success. We need *you* to be a success."

Watts offered me a cheery expression but I rejected the sentiment. If ever a time called for sincerity, it was that moment.

* * *

The Research Hub was abandoned from eight in the evening to eight in the morning. Any staff still on duty took their casework elsewhere, opting for the comfort of their cottage over the vast emptiness of that dimly lit, clammy space. As any time spent in my accommodation was mere foreplay to sleep, I preferred to set up camp in the Hub.

That evening, I reread the WORM report and attempted to create a psychological timeline from David as a healthy child to an adult in need of relief. Key psychological issues always stem from childhood, with the most common motives derive from a lack of physical, mental or emotional development. This can be caused by abuse or negligence early on in life, yet David had a fairly privileged childhood. The only abnormal behavioural changes arose in adulthood after he inexplicably stopped going to work and cut all contact with family and friends. In the report, his colleagues and neighbours described him as defiantly unresponsive rather than vacant, troubled or confused, so his need for relief seemed more of an erratic decision rather than a solution to a longstanding problem. It wasn't exactly the behaviour of someone nearing desistance.

After reading for just a couple of hours, a rhythmic thump erupted across the front of my head, indicating the need for a different approach. I rubbed my eyes, pushed the headphones deep into my ears and pressed play on the interview footage, my fingers positioned above the keyboard and ready to take notes.

"Any reason why you're asking me this?"

David looked sicker on screen than he had in person. His speech was slurred. His neck didn't look strong enough to hold the weight of his head.

"We need to establish your past before we can proceed with your future. Knowing more about you will help us figure out the best way to tackle your case. Please answer my question: is money an issue with you? As you don't work, who supplies you with food? With money for your bills?" "You're going to make this a really boring talk. There's not much to say."

"Who's Trent?"

I rewound the footage a few seconds.

"You're going to make this a really boring talk. There's not much to say."

"Who's Trent?"

I rewound again.

"Who's Trent?"

I hit pause and took my headphones off. I was sure the door had just opened behind me, but when I turned everything in the room remained dark and still.

As I faced the screen again a heavy thud echoed through the Hub. It had come from outside.

I walked over to the window, trying to locate the source of the noise, but my view was restricted by the metal bars and safety plastic. Eventually, by positioning my head to the left and peering downwards at an odd angle, I found that I could just about see the grounds below.

A small group of men had somehow managed to get onto the grounds. I recognised a few of them as regular protesters and, although the majority of them were clearly panic-stricken, two men at the front were wearing expressions of complete exuberance. One nodded to the other and a rock was pelted at the wall metres below where I stood.

I'm not sure what they hoped to achieve, and I doubt even they really knew, but their chances of causing any real damage ended seconds later as the security guards slithered behind them in quiet formation. A few of the men in the group instinctively felt their presence and tried to escape, but they were quickly dragged away by dark gloved hands, their bodies slacking as they were hauled towards a vehicle that had somehow appeared unnoticed from the shadows.

Gradually the protesters were picked off one by one, until only the two most defiant men remained. They taunted the uniformed guards, gesticulating and jumping about wildly while throwing rocks and sticks.

Without warning, two thin lines of glinting silver shot out from the direction of the guards, impaling one protester in the forehead and the other in the shoulder. They both began to violently jolt and writhe, their heads flinging back as their arms seized stiffly at their sides. Eventually, they collapsed to the floor to judder and quiver as the two thin lines detached and slid back to their owners.

One security guard broke rank and walked toward the man who had been hit in the shoulder. He calmly raised a booted foot and dug the heel hard into the twisted, unconscious face.

I saw no blood as the foot was removed, only a sunken shape where the nose had been.

# 11

The physical examinations took place on the floor above the morgue. It was deemed imperative that the close proximity between these two areas was kept quiet, which was surprisingly easy to achieve despite both floors being below ground level and only accessible via a specific lift.

David eyed the lift's three buttons but said nothing as it began to grind slowly downwards. Its sluggish movement and tinny groans were occasionally interrupted by spasmodic judders, a unique movement that the sweeps – the lift's most frequent users – often seemed to emulate.

The metal box settled with a clang and the doors squealed open to reveal a ward almost identical to every other in the facility. The only distinction was its emptiness, accentuated by an abandoned reception area and an upturned chair.

My rubber plimsolls made a satisfying clack as I led the way down the corridor. Each room we passed was intended for physical examinations, training and emergencies, but most served as storage space for surplus equipment. Every so often a sweep or cleaner would scuttle past like a disturbed woodlouse but staff tended to avoid the area, perhaps due to the instinctive reasoning that any unoccupied space is best kept away from.

Despite irregular use, every room on the floor was sterilized daily. As I pushed open the door to one of the stark white examination rooms I felt a mild burning sensation in my nostrils from the chemical fumes. Everything I touched was tacky from numerous layers of cleaning products.

I stepped aside to allow the phys aid to lift David onto the examination table, although he managed to climb up most of the way himself before his weak arms began to buckle. The most recent phys aid report mentioned a reduction in wheezing and an improved ease in walking, but until that point it hadn't struck me how much stronger he had become in such a short amount of time.

Once on the table, David began to fidget. "So what are we waiting for?" he asked. He looked between the phys aid and I with a smile that didn't quite reach his eyes. "Which one of you has the joy of seeing my naked body?"

The new surroundings were clearly making him nervous. It must have looked completely different from anything he had seen so far in the facility; the medical instruments were not hidden in concealed drawers, and there were monitors covering every inch of the walls and ceiling showing images of beaches, woodlands and fields. They were supposed to evoke a sense of calm before the examination, after which point they would project a live feed of the patient from the array of cameras directed at the table. Most patients closed their eyes to it eventually, unaccustomed to seeing themselves from such unforgiving angles.

"We don't perform the physical examination." The phys aid grinned, thrilled to have possessed sufficient knowledge to answer the question. “We’re just witnesses. A specialist doctor will be coming here soon to do it.”

“He’s late,” I said.

“Only by a few minutes.”

“According to my e-Noter he’s not even in the building yet.”

“I’ve messaged him,” she said, her eyes seeming to widen with each syllable, “he should be here any minute now.”

“But he won’t be here any minute if he’s not in the building, will he? It takes twenty minutes alone to get through security and to sign off on his pass. Then he has to find his way down here. Go and look for him, or at least find out when he’ll arrive. This room is only booked for so long.”

“Look for him?”

“Yes. This is valuable time being wasted.”

“So you want me to...”

“I want you to go upstairs, ask patient services, speak to reception on the main floor, message security and *look* for him.”

“I could just message them from here.”

I swallowed my initial response. “You know they won’t reply.”

With no more excuses left in her arsenal, the phys aid moved slowly toward the door as if I might change my mind if she gave me the chance. I held her gaze until she edged out of the door and closed it softly behind her.

“Wow,” David said, “that was excruciating.”

“Indeed,” I said.

Because the black in David’s hair was fading and his deep brown roots were beginning to show, a warmth of colour was beginning to emerge in his complexion. I was confident he would pass the physical examination, and with Logue MIA it seemed as though my chances of proving desistance were finally beginning to look a little better.

"So what happens now?" David asked.

"We wait," I said, sitting down on one of the plastic chairs lined up against the wall.

"No, I meant during this thing. What's going to happen?"

"Haven't your phys aids gone through this? It's a physical examination. You'll be..."

"Examined physically, I get that much, but what actually happens? What are they looking for?"

The words rose up from my memory and spewed out of my mouth without any mediation with my brain, "Today a doctor, your phys aid and I will be present at your physical examination. Your phys aid and I will stand as witnesses as the doctor assesses your overall health by performing numerous scans and tests. This is to ensure your physical condition is not having an impact on your decision to be at Boar House, and neither will it become a hindrance to any treatment we may later provide. The examination will take approximately three hours. The doctor will explain each test and answer any questions you may have before he begins. Most of the results are immediate but we will discuss them with you after the doctor and I have analysed them first. This may take two to three working days. If you're deemed physically healthy and your request for relief is not a physiological side effect, you will continue with the process. If there are any discrepancies, your case will be taken to an external mediator."

*And if it all goes wrong you'll be taken to a psychiatric facility and held there for the rest of your life, so let's hope it all works out okay.*

David nodded slowly. "So all three of you will be here. While I'm naked."

"Yes."

"And it's invasive."

"Yes."

"Painful?"

"I'd say more uncomfortable than painful."

"I love when doctors say things like that."

"I'm a euthanasist, not a doctor."

"Whatever. I just meant you should try being poked and gawped at before you have an opinion on whether it hurts or not."

"I have been."

He leaned back, his eyes narrowed. "Really?"

"Yes."

"When? Why?"

"All euthanasists have to submit to a full physical examination before training. There's also two weeks of psychological assessments to pass in order to graduate."

It was fairly satisfying to watch his defiance dissipate. He adopted a softer expression, perhaps believing we now had something that connected us together. It's strange how human beings are so desperate to cling to familiarity that they bypass all other differences.

"So what's it like?" he asked, pulling his spindly legs close to hug his knees.

"It's just a series of tests, it's more tedious than anything."

"Were you nervous before you had yours?"

The echoes of vulnerability could be heard in his voice. He couldn't bring himself to look me in the eye but was clearly eager for an answer.

"Yes," I said.

"What were you most nervous about?"

I considered ignoring his question to offer the usual comforting words recited to patients during such situations – about how the medical team would deem his naked body as nothing more than a puzzle to solve– but he was being honest. I felt the urge to do the same.

"I didn't want them to ask about my scars."

"What scars?"

I showed David my left hand, and the middle, ring and little finger that are crooked and lined with thick white and pink scars. His own hand moved to touch the damaged tissue, but he thought better of it and pulled back.

"How did that happen?"

I hadn't thought about it for so long that I struggled to recall the event at first, but eventually the day I ran away from my foster parents came back with surprising clarity.

I was in the midst of being confirmed a trainee euthanasist, a process that involved weeks of home confinement while I underwent background checks. I was happy to comply at first, but within days Mr and Mrs McCall became relentless in their mission to change my mind and subsequently withheld many privileges from me. With nothing to pass the time I found myself becoming increasingly agitated. Escaping the house for the afternoon seemed the least damaging option of the many I had considered.

As I climbed down from my bedroom window it seemed like dozens of people were walking past the house, yet none of them were concerned by the fact that I was outside. Their indifference spurred me on and I began to dodge the bodies, my gait quickening to a jog as I made my way towards the community park.

It was a grim location – a few rusty swings on soft tarmac within a metal penned area – but at least it was empty. I didn't notice the paint-chipped gates scratch my hands as I opened them, nor the ripped skin flaking from my palms as I hurried forwards; my focus was set entirely on the set of swings in front of me, the left one in particular. It had the least amount of cracks on the rubber seat.

I sat gently, my feet coming off the ground despite being almost sixteen years of age. I had always been shorter than the other children at school, with rounded flesh that sat awkwardly on my slight frame.

The guilt began to ferment in my gut as I swung slowly back and forth. Mr and Mrs McCall would be arrested were I caught outside their property, and their son Henry would be swallowed whole by any children's home that took him in, but I couldn't go back. Not straight away. It had been such a long time since I had been allowed to enjoy solitude. I hadn't even been able to walk unaccompanied to my classes at school, or been left to sleep for an entire night without being checked on. It was as if I was on suicide watch, which was irritatingly ironic.

Still, it wouldn't be long before I was free of it. Free and away from everything. I wouldn't have to persuade people that I knew my own mind and was making the right decision to become a euthanasist, because I would be self-sufficient. I had so many plans and ambitions that it became an energy burning inside me.

I just needed those five minutes alone in the park before facing the final few days in that house. I would return without being noticed and be able to get on with my life.

Because that's what I would be getting. A life.

"Nieve?"

I had been found. Six of my ex-classmates entered the park. I felt nauseous– no one was supposed to see me in person other than my guardians. I looked for an exit but there was only the one gate.

"Don't worry, we're not going to say anything to anyone," one of the girls said. I think her name was Debbie, but as I hardly knew her I didn't know whether to feel comforted or alarmed by her words. I stood slowly and tried to figure out how I could get past her to the gate.

The rest of my ex-classmates spread out across the park. One of the boys kicked a can to the left of me and I jumped. A girl near him giggled, apparently greatly amusedly by this.

Debbie sat on the swing next to me, pushing herself backwards with her toes and dragging her heels across the tarmac as she came forward. "When do you head off?"

"What, home?"

Debbie snorted and the others followed suit. They were circling the park, their collective laugh like a delayed echo. "No, you idiot, when do you go off for training?"

I shrugged, taking a small step away from the swing. "In about a week."

"Just having your last bit of freedom until you're locked up for the rest of your life, then?" she said, a smattering of malice in her words.

"I won't be locked up. I'll be allowed out."

"Not without permission."

I shrugged again and glanced at the gate.

Debbie got up to stand on the seat of the swing. She was incredibly tall and thin with an almost freakishly long face and had a nose that protruded like a hook, yet despite her prominent features she was captivating, almost beautiful. I, with my rounded body and small eyes, have always looked like a petulant child.

She jumped off the swing. Her smile disappeared.

"You have five seconds."

A heat radiated from my abdomen and spread to my neck. "What?"

Her fists were clenched and shaking.

"You have five seconds to get out. Five... four..."

I thrust my foot out to start running, but it got caught and I fell hard onto my hands and knees. I looked back to see the boy who had kicked the can had his leg extended. He began laughing. A girl beside him imitated his cackle.

As I tried to push myself up, Debbie lifted her foot high in the air and stamped down onto the back of my left hand. The crack of the bones reverberated up my arm and rattled my ribs. As the pain shot up through to my shoulder, my throat constricted into a silent scream. I instinctively scrambled onto my haunches and cradled my arm, trying to protect the three fingers that stuck out, quivering.

I tried to stand again but was pushed onto the ground and the back of my head bounced hard against the tarmac. All six of them encircled and peered down at me.

I felt anger beyond anything I had experienced before, but this was quickly overtaken by fear – fear of being hurt again, fear of the McCalls being imprisoned, fear of losing my opportunity to be taken away from it all.

Debbie let a globule of saliva slowly trickle out of her mouth and splatter onto my forehead. "That's for my uncle. He was in a mental home and they had him put to fucking sleep like a dog. He was forty-seven. Does that make you feel good? You excited to do that sort of shit to people?"

I stayed quiet. Whatever I said would have worsened the situation, even if I was to tell her that it was likely her family had requested her uncle's relief.

As I lay there wondering how and when it would all end, one by one they spat fat, fleshy balls of phlegm onto my face. Once the giggling girl had let her watery dribble splash onto my chin, they exited the park.

"Nieve?"

I was slumped on the plastic chair with David leaning over me. All I could see was mottled skin and bones. I closed my eyes to try and alleviate the queasiness.

"I think you fainted. You were mumbling. Are you okay?"

"Yes. Fine."

A hollow feeling had begun to assert itself in my stomach. I realised I hadn't eaten at all that day – the cafeteria was used by patient's families, making it a hazardous minefield for questions, hysterical bargaining and emotive outbursts. I often avoided it.

"Are you sure you're okay? Shall I call for someone?"

I breathed in deeply, holding my throbbing, scarred hand close to my chest.

"They always find out in the end," I said, my mind in several places at once.

I don’t why I had said it, but it made David grapple for lost words and buried thoughts. The arrival of the doctor and phys aid ended his fight for speech.

# 12

"When did this happen?"

"I don't know."

"And this right here?"

"What about it?"

"Who did it to you?"

"I did it to myself, I just can't remember when."

"But the thing is, David, judging from the angle someone else must have done it to you."

"I did it to myself."

I zoomed in on the footage of David's left thigh. The shiny, pink bubbles of scar tissue could not have been more than a few months old. Doctor Fisher prodded it gently with a gloved hand.

"How did you do it?" he asked, lowering his face to inspect it closely. It was one of the many scars that littered David's body.

I hit pause. I had been studying the examination footage from the moment the doctor had left the facility until piercing yellow light had glinted through the blinds the following morning. I had rewatched once to familiarise myself with the findings, a second time to bookmark the most important sections and god knows how many other times to flit back and forth between relevant points. I planned to go back to my cottage once I had finished taking notes on the correlation between David's physical, vocal and emotive responses, but my brain had already been numbed by the repeated viewings and I struggled to type anything coherent.

And yet I couldn't leave, my desperation to complete the report compelling me to watch again and again and again.

I skipped through the clips of the doctor measuring, photographing and cataloguing the scars (each of which David attributed to self-harm) and played the twelve-minute analysis of David's malnutrition.

"You've created a lot of issues for your body by starving yourself," Doctor Fisher had said as he gestured for David to step onto the scales, "some of it may even be permanent. Did you know that?"

David sniffed. "That doesn't really matter now, does it?"

Despite gaining a noticeable amount of weight since arriving, David was still only one hundred and twenty pounds. He wasn't able to see the display but he shuffled off the platform quickly, no doubt reading the look of shock on the phys aid's face as the figure appeared on her e-Noter.

The doctor helped him back onto the table. "It seems a bit silly to just stop eating, more attention-seeking than anything. A cry for help."

David pushed the doctor's hand from his bare shoulder. "It wasn't about getting attention."

"Oh no? So were you trying to kill yourself? Or did you feel you needed to lose weight?"

"Of course not."

"Why did you do it then?"

When David failed to answer the doctor replied for him, “You did it to hurt yourself. To punish yourself. Am I right? To make yourself feel pain. What have you done that’s so bad you felt the need to punish yourself like this, hmm?”

David looked away.

Doctor Fisher exhaled loudly, and I realised I’d been holding my own breath for quite some time. “You clearly aren’t very happy being you. It’s a lucky thing you’re here, it’s not good to take these sorts of matters into your own hands. Whether you made these scars yourself or someone else did them to you, I can tell you feel as though you deserve them. That’s why you won’t tell me how you got them, isn’t it? This is something I’m sure your euthanasist will want to talk about later.

“Anyway,” he said, reading a syringe to take another blood sample, “let’s move on to your immune system, shall we? How often do you come down with colds, would you say?”

Doctor Fisher had an incredibly enviable talent of extracting information conversationally, benefitting the case more in hours than Logue had managed in weeks. The footage of he and David coupled with a few focussed psychological assessment transcripts may have even been enough for the case to pass at committee, but only if I attempted to hide the inconsistencies. His apartment, the avoidance of his family…it was just too much to palm off as inconsequential. And how could I pass up such a perfect opportunity to prove desistance?

I couldn’t take any more. I turned the screen off, rubbing my painfully dry eyes until they felt like they were a part of my skull again.

Six hours later, I awoke in my cottage to discover Watts had granted me a day's leave. I was to see where David had been living for the past few years and potentially interview his parents, time permitting. I knew instinctively that it was going to change everything.

I had to be taken via MediTaxi, the vehicles used to transport patients. For non-patient, non-emergency trips the MediTaxi technicians often took multiple passengers to save on resources. It made every journey significantly longer than it should have been, but thanks to an unusual bout of luck I was the only passenger that day.

The roads themselves were another problem altogether. With officials posted every two miles it was impossible to get anywhere without travel passes being scanned half a dozen times. The officials always apologised, saying they were only there for public safety, what with so many public service vehicles being hijacked during the travel crisis, but I think they were more concerned for the protection of government property.

As I left my cottage and walked towards reception, it dawned on me that I hadn't left the facility since I had started working there – just over three years before. Without friends or family beyond the gates there hadn't been any reason for me to go to the considerable effort to leave, and during my free time I occupied myself by either walking the grounds or working in the Hub. I have met many people who have expressed confusion, pity or even disgust at the lengthy periods I remained at Boar House, some even claiming I was somehow unknowingly institutionalised. These sorts of people view their own lives as freer than mine despite its repetitive, mundane structure, simply because they have been able to permit themselves moments of nothingness. To them, time wasted with people they neither like nor care about is a right, and I'm oppressed not to have experienced it, but why must I pour away hours of my life just because I can?

The woman who worked at reception was definitely one of those people. As I filled out the paperwork for my travel pass she chattered about people and things and events, not giving a damn about who I was and clearly happy to have an excuse not to work. All I could focus on was the greying roots pushing through the dark blonde dye she used far too seldom.

"Going anywhere nice?" she asked.

"Not really," I said. Sensing she was displeased with my response, I added, "It's just work-related. Should be a nice day for it, though."

She grinned enthusiastically.

"It does! It looked a bit cloudy earlier but it's definitely getting sunnier. And warmer. It'll be summer before we know it, won't it? Well, anyway, back to the boring stuff. I just have to make you aware that the facility is not liable for anything that happens to you outside of the grounds. Our insurance only extends to the end of the drive, so if you have any issues please speak to the local authorities as we won't be able to come and get you or help in any way. We're also not legally obligated to give you advice or send or receive any data while you're out. Your driver has insurance, but please note this only extends to situations involving the vehicle itself.

"If you share confidential information concerning the facility, our staff members or our patients to civilians, your contract will be immediately terminated and we will hand you over to the authorities. A minimum prison sentence for such an act I believe is five years…but it may be longer now, I can never keep up with these things!

"You should have applied and received your civilian money by now, but if you haven't you can borrow some from the petty cash box. In the event of your death, your next of kin will be notified and given authority over your body as well as any investigations that may have to take place. If you have no next of kin it will fall under the jurisdiction of the police. Please make sure to keep your tracker switched on at all times for the purpose of our files.

"And I think that's it! Have a good day and a safe journey, my lovely."

I mirrored her smile, which seemed to involve an excessive movement of my cheeks, and left through the main entrance.

Beyond the frosted glass doors a burst of aggressive cheer engulfed me. The protesting crowd had engorged overnight, almost spilling out onto the road as the security guards waded through them, shouting and prodding at anyone in their way. Watts had mentioned that their numbers had become a problem but to see them, to feel the warmth radiating off so many bodies amassed together was another thing entirely.

It was only as I walked down the stairs and through the car park that I realised the space reserved for my MediTaxi was empty; the vehicle was still submerged in the crowd, the security guards having failed to prise off the protesters clinging to the bonnet. It inched forward uneasily but had to stop two metres away from the front gates with seemingly no way of passing through the squirming net of intertwined bodies.

A security guard flapped his arms at me and motioned toward a side gate at the far left of the driveway, indicating for me to unlock it and clamber through the crowd in order to get to the vehicle. I was hesitant, justifiably fearing for my safety, but the longer I waited the more furiously the man waved and mouthed indecipherable instructions.

I mistyped the code twice before the gate unlocked and the latch fell sideward. The nearby protesters stepped back to let me through at first, but after a few steps they quickly closed in.

It was difficult to focus, difficult to even make out my own feet amongst the dozens of legs shuffling about me. I was swaying to and fro as if battling against a current. Trying to move in a straight line was exhausting and I was trodden on, tapped, tugged, touched, pulled...

And then the questions and chants began, the noise spreading and surrounding me like fire on dry wood.

"Where is she going?"

"Cure, don't kill! Cure, don't kill!"

"Who's that one?"

"That's Nieve Hindeman– where you going, Nieve?"

"Do you do home visits now? Taking people from their fucking homes?"

"Monsters!"

"Cure, don't kill!"

"How can you live with yourself?"

"What's it like being paid to murder vulnerable people?"

It was impossible to block everything out. Hands began to jab at me and wave in front of my face, threatening to do more than simply remind me I was surrounded, and the consequential adrenaline flooding my bloodstream made it difficult to walk calmly onward. I kept my eyes low, not wanting to look at anyone directly in case it instigated something.

It felt like hours had passed by the time I reached the car. The relief of feeling the cool handle against my fingertips drained me in an instant. I got in slowly to seem calm and in control, but my entire body was shaking.

Palms began to bash against the windows. Infuriated muffled shouts grew louder. The driver held onto the horn as we reversed.

"I bet you're putting all these mentals on your waiting list," the driver said, sighing. "No one would care if you put them down. A complete waste of space. All of them."

I said nothing, hoping he'd remain silent for the rest of the journey.

* * *

We bounced up onto the pavement, the car lurching as the driver braked. The only activity that had occupied me for the last three hours was the view outside the window, but my muscles ached as if I had run for miles.

"You know where you're going, I take it," the driver said.

I checked my e-Noter. The image on the screen was the same tall, sandy-coloured building that stood in front of us, and the map confirmed we were at the correct location. "Apartment 325. And the parents' place is just a fifteen-minute walk away."

He laughed through his nose. "Well, you're obviously not going to walk there. I'll be waiting to take you once you're done."

"Why can't I walk there by myself?"

He looked at me through the rear view mirror, his mouth stretched into an impatient sneer.

"I have to take you."

"Why?"

"Jesus. When was the last time you were out?"

I decided not to answer.

"You can't walk that far on your own. Just come back here when you're done and I'll drive you. I'm not going anywhere. We don't want another Miller Park, do we?"

His need to feign concern irritated me. I opened up the car door and stepped out, assuring my return with a swift nod.

The colour of the apartment block looked unintentional as I got up close, as if its shade was the result of an enormous tea stain. Even the front garden seemed murky, with stippled brown, scraggly plants bordering a path made of washed-out yellow stones, but the jaundiced grass was carefully mowed and the dead leaves had been swept into a neat pile. Someone had clearly tried, but you can't repair a scratched surface simply by polishing it.

It felt wrong entering the building and ascending its lift without the use of codes, cards or scanners. As I reached the fifth floor I clutched my travel pass tightly, wondering how the interior had managed to remain relatively undamaged despite a complete lack of security. The parks and public buildings I had visited as a child were always covered in graffiti or disfigured in some way. There was an unmistakable dinginess about the place, but nothing in that apartment building had been deliberately tampered with – and yet the fact that it hadn't been touched somehow made it even shabbier.

The lift doors parted and the floor was silent except for a low, electrical hum. I almost managed to convince myself I was alone in an empty building; I couldn't imagine any of the doors I passed holding homes behind them, places in which people felt comfortable enough to live and eat and sleep. The cottage at the facility may have been small and ridiculous-looking but it was private, familiar. With so many identical apartments practically on top of one another it felt like they held more of a formal purpose, like storage rooms or lockers.

I knew which apartment was David's long before I was able to make out the metal numbers nailed above it. The door was freshly painted, the same emerald green colour as the rest of the floor only more vivid, and the doorknob was a glistening gold, not scuffed and dull like the others.

The key felt heavy and primitive in my hand. I was surprised at how easily it slid into the lock, the latch releasing with only the slightest pressure. As the door opened a waft of bitter chemicals and artificial fragrances was released, clawing at my throat and stinging my eyes, but once the fumes had cleared I was able to see just how thorough the WORM report had been; every corner, every object and every angle seemed immediately familiar to me.

I walked around, running my hand across the white worktops that encircled the living space as if I had done it every day, and in the corner where the cheap laminate made way for white linoleum in the kitchen area my false memories felt the change in texture before my feet did.

As the place had already been checked for prints I was able to touch every unused switch, button, handle and latch. The walls and furniture were cold, smooth, clean and untainted, not a rough or sharp surface in the whole place.

It was all a stage.

I walked past the pale blue bathroom and into the bedroom. It was a small, square room with a double bed that took up most of the floor space. There were no sheets or pillows, only a mattress, but the room was a little more…real, I suppose. I've always struggled to describe the significance I saw in that room. It looked as though it was actually made for human habitation despite the continued smell of paint and chemicals. I'm not one to talk about anything beyond the tangible, but I sensed something in there that I hadn't in the rest of the apartment. Perhaps you can only clean so much life away.

It felt right to climb on top of the bed, just to see how it felt. The mattress was flimsy and dipped in the centre. No matter where I positioned myself I kept sinking back into the middle. It was no wonder David had such a poor posture.

Laying in the impression his body had made was a strange experience, as if I was there but somehow watching myself. Like in a dream. On some level I must have felt that patients only came into existence the moment they stepped into the front doors of the facility, their life before seeking relief nothing more than a story that others corroborated with. Lying in that space was important. A necessary part of the process yet unpleasantly intimate all at the same time. To think that he had been there for hours, for months, for years simply contemplating Boar House disturbed me. Perhaps he had researched euthanasists. Perhaps he knew about me before I had known about him.

My gaze was suddenly drawn to a dark patch in the corner of the otherwise pristinely white ceiling. I sat up, took my e-Noter out and flicked through the WORM report, but there was no mention of it anywhere. I tried to tell myself it was just damp coming from the floor above, but the longer I stared at it the more I convinced myself that it wasn't. It couldn't have been. There was no smell, no moisture in the air and the damage was isolated. It was in an almost perfect square shape.

I scrambled off the bed to fetch one of the white plastic bookshelves I had seen in the living room. They looked large and cumbersome but I was sure I could get one of them down and into the bedroom by myself to use as a makeshift ladder.

Pulling the bookshelf down and onto its side wasn't an issue, nor was pushing it through to the bedroom, but getting a grip on the smooth plastic shelves to lift it back up again was near impossible. It kept slipping and tearing the skin on my fingers. In the end I had to wedge my shoe beneath it just to get a hold of it. I could feel the sharp edges slicing across the top of my toes, but I ignored the stinging pain and somehow managed to haul it up and prop it against the wall.

It wasn't an ideal ladder. The shelves trembled threateningly as I slowly climbed up them one foot and one hand at a time, but it held. As I got nearer to the ceiling I was able to see the edging of the dark patch more clearly, which was far too neat to be organic.

While gripping tightly onto the bookshelf with one hand, I prodded the centre of the patch with the other. The dark square was like a bubble of dry, papery material that broke away easily from the rest of the ceiling and flittered to the floor. Dust billowed out after it in thick clouds, completely covering me in what looked like a grey white powder.

After the dust had settled I wiped my eyes with the inside of my uniform and looked up. A small square hole had been cut out of the ceiling. Someone must have tried to hide it by papering over it.

I reached up into the empty space and gently tapped at the edges with my fingertips. I quickly touched upon something plastic and crumpled that was small enough to grab and pull down.

In my hand was a dirty, transparent bag filled with dozens upon dozens of memory cards, each labelled with a unique number written in biro. I turned the bag over and saw the word 'MESSAGES' scribbled across it in faded black marker.

* * *

The house was absurdly narrow. The sole purpose of its unusual design must have simply been to fill the gap between the houses either side of it.

"Hello?" she said, peering around the door. I hadn't expected her northern accent to be quite as strong as it was.

"Mrs Myre? My name is Nieve Hindeman. I'm from Boar House."

Without saying another word she stepped back so I could come inside. She caught my elbow as she rushed to shut the door but didn't seem to notice.

There were no questions or invitations as I followed her through the hallway into the first room on the left, a small living room that was practically bare except for a couple of old floral-patterned armchairs and a battered coffee table. As I sat down I almost expected dust clouds to rise from the cushions. It certainly wasn't the sort of home I would have expected from a couple with a profession grade as high as her and her husband's.

Mrs Myre looked nothing like David. She had a short, fat nose where his was long and narrow, a rounded chin where his was sharp and thin mousey hair where his was thick and dark, albeit his was dyed. I wondered what his father looked like. Perhaps David looked exactly like him. Some people breed like cats, with half of their litter looking identical to the mother and the other half identical to the father, but David had no siblings I could compare him against.

I began to wonder whether I had siblings– or half siblings, which was more likely since my mother had died young from natural causes brought about by unnatural means and I had never known my father. Which of my parents was I more like? Maybe, unlike David, I was an even mixture of both.

Those thoughts soon bored me.

"You can't be long," Mrs Myre said suddenly.

"Okay," I replied, setting my e-Noter to record and placing it on the coffee table.

She sat very stiffly, her hands clawed into the arms of the chair. She continually glanced behind me to the bay window that looked out onto the street.

"I gather you know who I am and why I'm here?" I asked. She nodded. "I'm just trying to get to know David, to try and find out how we can help him. Did he tell you he was admitting himself into a relief facility?"

"No. But I found out."

"Were you surprised?"

"No."

I waited for more but was forced to prompt her. "Why not?"

"He was always like that."

"What do you mean?"

"I don't know. Sad. Quiet."

"What was he like as a child?"

"The same. Quiet. He didn't talk much."

Morose I might have accepted. Glum, moody, sarcastic or even aggressive at one point in his life, but quiet? Sad? Was she merely using these simplistic descriptions because she thought that was what I wanted to hear?

"Could you describe a time when you think he was particularly sad?"

"I... I can't think right now, you probably have to go soon."

I turned to look out of the window she was watching so intently. There was nothing and no one outside, just another row of houses staring straight back at us, separated by a potholed road.

"Is Mr Myre here?"

"No. He'll be back in a while."

"Does he know about David?"

"No. Well, he does, but he doesn't want to know."

So it was the husband creating all the panic. For whatever reason, she clearly didn't want him to find me in the house or speak with me, but I wasn't about to waste the opportunity to ask more questions. I couldn't afford to.

"We've had some trouble finding things out about David," I said, trying to get her full attention but losing once again to the view of the street. "His medical records for instance – for some reason they're incredibly vague. His school records are poorly written and even the therapist reports prior to his admittance are fairly inconclusive. We are undertaking physical and psychological assessments but I fear this may not be enough to help him in time."

Her blank face made me feel as though I had an itch I couldn't reach.

"Do you think your son should be given relief?"

Her eyes slowly panned down from the window and settled somewhere on my left shoulder. "Yes. He wants it."

"I could really use your help. And I promise, I'll be gone as soon as I have everything I need. Do you know how the relief system works?"

"Mostly."

"Okay, that's great. So overall we have a good case, but my job is to provide indisputable evidence that David needs relief. A few things have come up that seem a little odd to me, and I need to investigate absolutely everything to prove to the committee that he's really meant to be there."

"What do you need me for?"

"I just need you to answer my questions. It would be even better if you could forward any paperwork I don't have, or show me some of his belongings so I can get a better sense of what he's really like."

"We don't have anything of his."

"Nothing?"

"We got rid of it all years ago. He cut all ties. We both did."

"Why?"

She shook her head quickly, and I found myself mirroring her by gripping the arms of my chair.

"You got rid of everything? Absolutely everything?"

"It was his father's decision. David was difficult... it was the last straw."

"What do you mean, he was difficult?"

"We didn't get on."

"Why?"

"We just didn't. We don't know anything about him."

"You can't tell me anything? Maybe an example of what he was like?"

"I feel like I've never had a son. I know nothing about him. I didn't know him well before and I don't know him at all now."

I forced myself to inhale slowly. "Do you know his friend Valerie? Valerie Harmon?"

"No."

"Trent Williams?"

"No, I've never heard that name."

"When was the last time you spoke to David?"

She stood up and her small, fat fists were balled so tightly her knuckles turned white. Her eyes were shut and I half expected her to start screaming, or at the very least begin to cry, but instead she shuffled forward to get a better look out of the window.

"You have to go soon," she said, gently moving the net curtains aside.

"Yes, Mrs Myre, I know, I just need to ask you some final questions."

"Be quick, I've got things to be getting on with."

I moved the e-Noter closer to her, worried her voice was too soft to be clear on the recording. "Do you know anything about David's apartment?"

"I haven't a clue where he lived."

"Okay, how about his weight? Did you know he…"

"I told you, I haven't seen him."

"But if you don't care about him at all, why have you given him so much money over the years? You could have just allowed him to become homeless, but instead you paid all of his bills."

"I care about him," she said, her voice breaking slightly as she turned away from the window to face me, "how could I not care about him? I love him. He's my son. I just don't understand him, I don't understand him at all. I don't understand him or know who he is, or what he does or why, I just don't. I don't know anything and I won't say anything, so don't ask me, I just…he said… I just don't know anymore. We gave him money because he's our son. It was better than the alternative. It was all we could do. Now he's doing the right thing and I don't regret helping him because he really needed us then."

"And he doesn't need you now?"

"No, he doesn't need me now."

"But why did you pay for someone to clean his apartment? Was that the last time you spoke to him? Why did he ask you to do that?"

As the tension left her body the tears she had held onto spilled from her eyes. She wiped them away absentmindedly and returned to the window.

"I don't know anything about his apartment."

I couldn't tell if she was lying or not, and I don't know if I even cared by that point.

"Thank you for your time, Mrs Myre," I said, pulling myself up from the armchair. I stopped the e-Noter recording and put it into my pocket.

"I'll see you to the door," she said.

I held up my hand. “No need, honestly. Thanks for everything, it was really helpful.”

Before I left I had a quick scout up and down the hallway, but all the doors were shut and there was nothing to see but peeling wallpaper and a ceiling light with no bulb.

No photographs, no furniture, no ornaments. Just lifelessness.

# 13

It was dark by the time I returned, and the MediTaxi was able to pass easily through the fading clusters of protesters. The evening air soothed my hot, tired eyes as I clambered out, although my thoughts remained exerted to numbness.

As I closed the entrance doors behind me and faced the semi-gloom of the empty reception area, the long shadows made the ceilings seem higher, the chairs thin and towering. The awkwardly placed plastic chandelier hung overhead like a clawed hand reaching down toward me. It was only in this lighting that Boar House, which was ageless, featureless and plain in the day, contorted into something else, something beyond its simple, functional design.

I stood there for some time, aching and weak, waiting for some form of innate response to assume control and take me somewhere. When I eventually stumbled forward, it wasn't toward the cottages or the Hub, but to David's room.

There were no passing thoughts other than a passive acknowledgement of my destination. My hands automatically typed in the codes as I permitted my feet to find their way to the department, the rhythmic sway of my arms pulling me into an almost trance-like state. I don't remember passing anyone on the way, but as all of my energy was focussed on remaining upright I could have walked by a herd of phys aids and not have noticed.

When I reached his room it was as if I had been violently torn from a dream. I felt disorientated, with one foot raised off the ground frozen mid-step, suddenly overtly aware of my surroundings and the eyes of the night staff lurking behind the security cameras. Perhaps it was tiredness, but I was completely unable to bring any form of conclusion to my thoughts. Should I leave? Should I go into his room? What had I intended to do? Why, with a bag full of evidence that I was desperate to look through, had I even contemplated seeing the patient? He was the one element of the case that was proving a waste of my working hours.

David was sitting up in bed, still dressed in crumpled daywear and staring expressionlessly at nothing in particular. His thick hair hung in front of his eyes and he repeatedly batted strands away with clumsy, lethargic swipes. I had heard from staff that he slept very little, remaining practically motionless for hours until disturbed for tests or other activities. He had declined all offers of books, games and films from the facility library, preferring to exist with as little stimulus as possible.

It was hard to believe his weathered, sickly skin had ever looked healthy or youthful. I read a journal once (admittedly not a particularly science-based journal) that said VDA patients tend to look unhealthier after admittance as the emptiness they hold goes beyond a mere physical or psychological manifestation; it actually becomes them, overtakes their past and future, and all that's left is a lifeless vessel perpetually stuck in present time awaiting relief. It was apparently my job to reanimate patients so the committee considered them alive enough to kill – but how could I reanimate David when I hadn't found any signs of life to begin with?

David had been right when he said he frightened me, but it wasn't because I pitied him. It was the fear of failure. The answers were never found by talking to the patients, and his presence at the facility was essentially a decoy for the truth.

But that didn't matter now I had the memory cards.

I no longer felt tired. My next shift was to start in ten hours, so I had enough time to see what the hell I had found in his apartment and still get at least four hours sleep. I began to jog down the corridor, desperate not to waste any more time than I already had.

I stumbled to a stop when I realised the lights were already on in the Hub. I immediately recognised the man sitting at one of the workstations by the thinning hair at the back of the head.

Logue was slouched forward staring at the screen, his fixation so intense I was able to open the door, walk in and stand behind him completely unnoticed. He was watching some old case footage (at least fifteen-years-old by the look of the uniforms worn by the psych aids) in which two civilians wept with their arms around each other while staff scuttled around a bed. The cries of the civilians were heartfelt yet too quiet to be tears of shock and distress, so I assumed a patient had or was about to receive relief that was long overdue. Logue came into shot with fuller hair, a slimmer frame and fewer lines etched on his face, and as he gently pushed a petite female psych aid aside I caught a glimpse of a small body on the bed. It was a child, but it was far too small to be healthy. It squirmed weakly.

Logue leapt forward to shut off the screen.

"What are you doing?" he asked, breathless. "Are you following me now?"

"Of course not. As far as I'm concerned you don't even work here. Was that one of your old patients?"

"That has nothing to do with you."

I shrugged and set down my rucksack at a nearby workstation, pulling out the evidence bag to begin rifling through its contents.

"What's that?"

"Nothing to do with you." I sighed. "They're memory cards."

"What's on them?"

"I have no idea."

Logue shuffled over to look at the clear plastic bag but I pulled it out of reach, not quite willing to share that much of the case with him yet.

"Where did you get it? Is it for the Myre case?"

"Yes. I found it in his apartment."

"The one the WORMS searched?"

"Yes."

"You know that's impossible. Someone must have planted it in there afterwards."

"No one has had access to the keys."

"Someone could have found a way in."

I had been able to stave off my aggravation up until that point, but his incredulousness proved too much.

"So you're saying someone broke in, bashed through the ceiling, planted evidence, fixed the door and left without anyone noticing?"

"Where did you find it?"

"The bedroom ceiling."

"How did you know it was up there?"

"There was a discoloured patch."

"That just doesn't make sense. Why hadn't the WORMS seen it?"

"Maybe they didn't lie down on the bed like I did."

"You were on his bed?"

"Focus, Logue, I don't think that's really what's important right now."

He mulled it over for a moment.

"Did you report it?"

"Of course. I catalogued the evidence on my way back and the WORMS are going to take another look at the apartment tomorrow, after which I expect another worthless report. In the meantime, I'm going to search through these cards and find out what the hell is on them."

There was another lengthy pause, his mind almost audibly whirring as he considered the facts. "What made you go to the apartment in the first place? Why did Watts let you go?"

"I asked. I wanted to see it for myself."

"And he let you take time out to leave the facility just for that? Why?"

"I don't know, sheer desperation? You've put the case weeks behind schedule. This is also my first VDA case, the patient is uncooperative and we've had numerous setbacks. I think he'd do anything to see this end successfully."

I was too exhausted to be around Logue – I could feel myself losing control, which I didn't need with so much work left to do. I fought between the idea of demanding him to leave or just leaving myself.

He perched on the edge of the desk. After clearing his throat, he said, "Put one in the machine. I want to see what's on them."

There was an unfamiliar urgency in his voice that I found myself instinctively reacting to. I pawed through the bag until I found the card labelled '1' and slotted it into the side of the machine. It took a few moments for the software to be recognised, but eventually a notification asked permission to open an unknown file.

It was a video file.

I clicked play.

In a pale blue room, which I later recognised to be the bedroom in David's apartment, there was an empty grey office chair facing the camera. There were sounds of scratching and frustrated grunts before a plumper-looking David stumbled into shot and sat down heavily, his eyes narrowing at something off screen. His skin looked smoother and pinker, his hair freshly dyed and recently cut.

It was him but it wasn't him – his movements and mannerisms were exactly the same yet slightly off, as if he was doing an impersonation of himself.

David chewed his inner cheek as he continued to stare off into the distance. For a moment I thought the footage was playing on loop, but then he looked directly at the camera with startling hostility. I fought the urge to look away.

"Hello," he said quickly. Then he was silent.

I felt so uncomfortable sharing his expressionless gaze with Logue that my eyes wouldn't focus, and I became painfully aware of my own breathing. And then, mercifully, David began to speak again.

"I'm in pain every day. Not physical pain. It's kind of like having pins and needles, but in my brain. It's not there all the time – it's a big rush that comes and goes and I can't predict when it'll happen or make it start or stop. When it's there it's all I think about, all the time. No one else can see why I'm uncomfortable. No one else can see what's going on inside of me. If I complain about it everyone says it's only silly pins and needles, it'll go away, everyone gets it from time to time – but they forget what it's like when *they* had it, how it can consume you. It's causing this headache, this fogginess... I can't concentrate on anything. Everything seems slow, and I can't grasp things or touch them. I've not got enough blood going through me and my limbs are jelly and my eyes can't focus. I'm stiff as well as numb, I can't move and sometimes I try to walk and end up falling. My legs won't move. They won't *move*.

"This is such a stupid metaphor. I'm just... I'm just not here. Yet I can't leave. I feel so angry I want to scream. So... that's all I wanted to say today. I'll check in again tomorrow."

David looked off screen again, his face screwing up in concentration. Then he walked forward and the screen went black.

"It's a diary," Logue said.

I opened the playback menu. It showed only 2% of the memory card had been viewed. That probably amounted to 0.00002% of the whole collection of cards

"I think he's reluctant to talk," I said, holding up the evidence bag, "because he's said it all already."

# 14

I managed a few hours of fractured sleep before returning to the Hub. Through bleary eyes I sat through two full memory cards, although there was nothing particularly interesting on either one of them. Just the utterances of a dull, depressed young man, overthinking and underdoing.

"I keep telling myself I'll get out of bed after counting to ten, then twenty, then thirty, and then I just stop counting. They sent me a warning from work yesterday. I thought getting that would make me feel something, scared or worried maybe, but it didn't. I don't feel anything."

There were no specific details given in these short, daily accounts. Just snatches of emotion, occasional anecdotes and strange, nonsensical analogies. He would compare his mental state to physical ailments, fictional characters or colours and shapes which, although demonstrably articulate, seemed completely disconnected from his actual life.

The diaries were always filmed in his bedroom, and from the look of the lighting it was usually during the evening. I watched his hair grow, become unruly and then completely disappear by the next entry, his unevenly shaved scalp distracting me from his monotonous, verbalised thoughts. The blackness of the hair was renewed at random, sometimes when the colour was only partially faded and other times when it had almost completely returned to its natural dark brown.

I skipped a few minutes of footage here and there, perhaps an hour or so at the most whenever he began another tiresome monologue. The subject matter was usually his relentless boredom or the details of an errand he would never carry out. His eyes grew vacant and his lips pursed slightly as the mundane nothingness juddered out of him like an engine failing to catch.

Lack of sleep eventually caught up with me. Blurred spots began to cloud my vision and my entire body ached, but as I leant forward to turn off the machine the next entry began to play. I hesitated – it seemed different to the others.

David emerged onscreen with an awkward shuffle, his left arm hanging stiffly by his side. He gulped back tears, his throat squeaking with the effort of containing them. Something had palpably changed in him. He seemed to have physically transformed, becoming smaller and thinner in the space of twenty-four hours.

"I couldn't handle things today," he finally managed to get out, continuing to gulp. He roughly scrubbed the wetness from his face with the back of a trembling hand. "I just... fuck, I really can't stop shaking. It's just... something happened and I wanted to show it on camera. I think it's important."

He slowly peeled back the long sleeve that covered his left arm, his face contorted into a wince. Once it was rolled up to his elbow he allowed a whoosh of air to escape his lips and angled his forearm toward the camera.

Along the smooth, pale skin of his arm were thick cuts running widthways in a long, tidy row, right up to the wrist. They were raw, swollen and raised, and he kept lifting his arm back up so he could look at them. After a while he was able to calm himself down.

"The skin feels really tight."

He gently pulled the sleeve back down and lowered his arm to his side. With a loud sniff he turned off the camera.

It didn't make sense.

David's mood had changed from consistently low and lethargic to frightened and self-destructive in mere hours. He was also clearly detached, as if his arm didn't belong to him. He may have been in shock but the behaviours just didn't seem to correlate.

And he said the self-harm was important, but for whom?

"You look like shit."

Logue sat down heavily at the workstation beside me and logged on. I instinctively grabbed the bag of memory cards and set them down by my feet, away from his line of sight.

"I've been working." I placed a hand over my heart to quieten its loud thumps. "There's a lot of memory cards to go through."

"Find anything?"

I'm not sure why, but I felt the need to play the last entry to him. I rewatched it with him in silence. As David pulled his sleeve back down on screen I expected to see the same intrigue, excitement and confusion in Logue that I had seen the day before, but in its place was his usual blank stare. His mouth was slightly open, reminding me of some of the older patients with their dead minds and warm bodies.

"Well?"

His lips barely moved as he replied, "I suppose it's just a case of trudging through the rest of the cards. If you find more of the same... well... that's that."

"What do you mean? That's that?"

"It looks like you've got everything you need. It's open and shut."

"Did you just see the same thing I did?"

He finally turned to me, his bloodshot eyes lifeless. "What do you want me to say? The committee now has evidence of depression and self-harm. You don't need me to say what that means."

"I want you to say you saw what I saw. The disparity in his psychological state before and after the self-harm makes no sense. It needs exploring. How do we even know he hurt himself? He's always denied it and we didn't actually see him do it, so maybe..."

"*Nieve.*"

I hadn't noticed him get up. He was suddenly by the door, already physically and mentally moving away from the case.

"Stop looking for something that isn't there," he said, his hand on the door handle."Finding the memory cards was exciting, but you can't let that get in the way of what's right in front of you. I get it, you're disappointed that there isn't anything more to this. I would be too. But the evidence is right there."

"Is it? He sounds like he's reading from a script half the time. This really doesn't feel right."

"It's not uncommon for VDA euthanasists to feel like that, but you'll drive yourself crazy if you keep looking for things that aren't there. This is going to happen whether you like it or not. You're not stopping the inevitable by doing this, you're just delaying it."

"I'm not trying to stop anything, I'm trying to work out why he's here. I don't get it, one minute you're telling me my assessments are too severe and the next you're telling me to ready the Coactucin."

"Me? You're acting on nothing more than a hunch. You can do and say what you want but with this amount of evidence, right or wrong, it's happening. No one on the board will dispute it, so I suggest you focus on finishing things up and stop dragging it out before you lose your job. Skim through the rest of the memory cards if you feel the need to, but you said yourself that David came to you seeking relief. You need to fulfil your patient's wishes."

"*Our* patient's wishes."

"Does that matter? You'll be the one completing the procedure. Watts is looking to you for this one. I'm not a part of it now."

"So that's it? You're done? The Harmons? Trent? The cleaners? You think that can all be brushed under the carpet?"

I could tell a part of him wanted to argue, but he was trying his best to let go of it. The influential man he had once been was well and truly gone.

"You need to get it done."

I sighed. "Fine. But I don't think you should tell him about any of this, just to be safe."

"Who? Watts?"

"No. David. Don't tell him we found the diaries."

"Why?"

"We need all the evidence we can get at committee, and if he thinks we have all the answers he'll become complacent. We still need him to spell things out for us."

He nodded, but we both knew I had only asked as a rather inept gesture of respect – he had no reason to speak with David anymore.

I was now officially working on my own.

# 15

I lay awake in my cottage that night, and with lack of sleep came disconnected thoughts. I could feel the air building in my chest as my mind went over each detail again and again and again. I was drowning in it, desperately in need of extra weeks, days, even hours. But David's time wasn't just governed by clocks and calendars. The only way I could complete the case properly and get enough information to prove desistance was to slow down what was perceived to be progress, but how could I prompt a setback? How could I weaken him?

Then it struck me: I could attend a care meeting.

There was never a need for euthanasists to participate in care meetings. They were usually around ten minutes long and conducted daily by the lead phys aid and psych aid to discuss patient progress and delegate written orders. But early the next morning I made sure I was the first one to arrive.

The meeting room chairs were arranged in a circle, which was the specified layout for team discussions. I made a small space so that I could stand – I knew if I allowed myself to rest in any way I'd succumb to the mounting weaknesses of my body.

The lead psych aid turned up shortly after me, the blond man with the prominent chin. He gave me a quizzical look but said nothing as he chose a chair directly in front of where I stood. Next, two men and a woman entered, their animated chatter dissipating immediately upon noticing me. Apathetic to their subject of conversation, I watched the door for the rest of the team.

It took a full five minutes for the last few stragglers to take their seats.

"I assume we're all here now," I said, clearing my throat. A couple of them nodded a confirmation.

"Is there a problem?" the lead phys aid, a fat woman with large dimples where the bones of her knees and elbows should have been, asked.

"I just want to hear how things are going."

"Oh really?" she said, flagrantly raising an eyebrow to the rest of the room.

I ignored the resultant shuffles and exchanged glances. "Can we begin with a progress report?"

The lead psych aid immediately began to detail David's mental state, hour by hour, minute by minute. Every sentence contained unnecessary and incorrectly used jargon, only for him to come to the conclusion that David was sarcastic, bored and unsociable. A few of his assistants commented on his therapy sessions but overall it was obvious that David wasn't giving them much to go on. And I told them as such.

"Oh no," the lead psych aid replied, "things have really progressed, particularly over the last few days. He finds it difficult to open up but we're making steady progress. He's fighting us but he's also listening to us. It's only a matter of time before we get a major breakthrough."

"And how exactly do you plan on getting this breakthrough?"

He picked up his e-Noter and the following week's therapy plan flashed up on the screen in my hand. I'd read it earlier but made a point of slowly scrolling through it again.

"This is quite intense," I said. "Most of the sessions are not only long but back-to-back. Have you scheduled time for reflection or rest?"

"Well, I feel this is the best approach for…"

"And what about the therapies I plan to lead? Where are they going to fit in? I'm going to need to cut back on a lot of this."

"I just think we're making so much progress with him. We're really getting through."

"From your notes it seems he's less responsive than he was when he arrived."

"*That* is the progress. The thoughtless, automatic answers he gave before were his way of pushing back. Now, he doesn't speak as much and is quite subdued, but soon he'll…"

"That's not going to help me much when I take the case to the committee, is it? I'll forward you a new schedule later today."

His Adam's apple bobbed as he swallowed hard. I prepared myself for a counterattack, but he simply replied, "Yes, Miss Hindeman."

I turned to the phys aid. "Can we hear your report now?"

She sat up straight, brushed her cropped blonde hair from her forehead and smoothed down her uniform. "Not a lot has changed in regards to his health," she said, "but he's put on a few pounds. His strength seems to be improving with each physio session and his muscle mass is definitely increasing, as is his stamina. He doesn't seem to have any lasting damage from the malnutrition."

The nutrition plan appeared on my e-Noter screen. He was being given six small meals a day, containing high levels of proteins, fats, phosphates, calcium and potassium. A chart to the side showed he was gaining at least three pounds a week on average, meaning he would be viable for relief in two to four weeks. It was an efficient approach for maximum weight gain.

"Is this his plan?"I asked."Is this what he's on at the moment?"

"Yes, he's been on that for the past fortnight."

"I've never seen it before, it's not what he was on when he arrived, is it? Did either Logue or I approve this?"

"No, we've just…"

"You've just decided to take the patient's wellbeing into your own hands."

She looked to her left and right, silently requesting for some form of backup. No one spoke.

"Logue created the original nutrition plan himself, if I'm not mistaken," I said. "I agreed with it when I was first introduced to the case and still do now. It's sufficient for safe, healthy weight gain."

The phys aid suddenly settled on a passing train of thought. "We didn't want to bother you with something as minor as his meal plan, that's why you weren't aware of the changes. After a discussion the team felt three standard meals a day wasn't enough and his weight gain would plateau if we didn't try something else. Our concern is that he won't be well enough when the case goes to committee and he'll be automatically dismissed. I apologise for not informing you sooner. We assumed you would agree with our decision."

"You assumed wrong."

This time her wordless plea for backup was answered.

"I'd have to agree with Jack on this one," the lead psych aid said.

"You would?" I folded my arms. "Are you going to make a formal complaint with Doctor Watts, then?"

"I don't think that's really necessary," he said, "we just..."

"Do you think I'm putting the patient's health at risk?"

"No, but…"

"But as you seem to doubt my decision-making skills I will tell you why I'm pushing for this. Logue has been at Boar House for almost thirty years and has had more experience than both you and I combined, particularly when it comes to VDA cases. He knows that if David puts on too much weight too quickly, there will be psychological ramifications that could prove detrimental to his progress and to his acceptance of relief. Something you would have known if you had taken the time to ask or do any research.

"I will be seeing David more often to ensure he's making sufficient progress, both physically and psychologically, and your time with him will be reduced. If I'm being honest, I don't think he's getting the care he needs from the team at the moment."

The room was still. It remained that way until we disbanded two minutes later. I watched them all file out slowly and quietly, knowing that the minute the door closed behind them the chatter would begin.

Some may consider it deceit, morally corrupt or even a complete disregard for the code of ethics, but I had to get more time from somewhere. Ultimately, this case was more important than David, my career, the phys aids, psych aids and even the authority of Watts. Proving desistance would benefit hundreds, possibly even thousands of future patients, and what was the cost? A slight reduction in food for a patient who had already voluntarily starved himself for months, if not years. I'm sure he would also welcome a break from his incessant therapy sessions.

I admit it. I went against everything I stand for. I lied to delay David's recovery, but the compromises I made that day I would not hesitate to make again. It was the right call to make.

# 16

Having more or less guaranteed myself some additional time on the case, I dedicated the next few days to watching David's video diaries.

The footage following his apparent self-harm was erratic. David made multiple entries per day, and he didn't seem to adhere to any particular pattern when it came to their length or the time at which they were filmed. He was also getting noticeably thinner and displayed periods of such ferocious anger his face would turn purple, every syllable sending flecks of spittle flying towards the lens.

"It's hard to remember a time when I wasn't in this fucking room. This is all I have, this room and me and my thoughts. This is all I have to look forward to every day. I can't go outside, I can't see anyone or do anything, and I wake up and everything is exactly the same as it was when I went to sleep. I go to bed sometimes just for something to do. I'm not even tired. I was in denial before when I thought things would get better. I know for sure they won't now. This is it, this is all there is, and it's fucking boring. It's awful and I hate it, I hate it, *I hate it.*"

Aside from the occasional outburst, David moaned constantly about his physical ailments. He claimed to suffer from chronic headaches, nausea, dizziness and disorientation, which I attributed to poor diet, dehydration and lack of exercise. Watching a man document his slow descent into malnutrition was dull viewing, and with each entry I felt increasingly despondent. He said nothing more of his self-harm, Valerie, his parents… *nothing* of relevance in the hours and hours of footage I sat through.

I particularly despised his 'never' lists. "I'll never be drunk, I'll never get married. I'll never have kids. I'll never ride a horse. I'll never leave the country. I'll never eat lobster. I'll never have a tattoo. I'll never make anything. Well, part from these diaries, and I fucking hate them."

And then, after wasting days watching the diaries with nothing to show for them, the date of Trent Williams' visit arrived. I wasn't exactly reluctant to leave the Hub, but it added yet another complication to proceedings.

When I arrived to accompany David to the visitation room, he was dressed in facility-issued daywear and was sitting at the edge of his bed in his usual hunched posture. The phys aids had combed his hair back to expose the lighter, naturally coloured roots. His boyishly styled hair, together with the daywear that resembled pyjamas and his thin frame, made him look more thirteen than thirty.

After spending so long studying him on the screen, it was a bizarre form of déjà vu to see him again in person.

"Long time no see," he said.

"I've been working on your case. There's a few details I had to look over, but I'll arrange more assessments soon."

He nodded. "So where's the other doctor?"

"You mean the other euthanasist? I'm heading up your case for the moment while Mr Logue works with some other patients."

He nodded again, apparently unfazed or perhaps unsurprised by Logue's absence. He pulled himself up to stand and, trembling from the physical exertion he had just displayed, held both arms out to steady himself as he moved slowly toward the window. That was the first time I had seen him walk unaccompanied. His legs were stiff and unsteady, but the physiotherapy was clearly working well for him. Of course, the reassigned nutrition plan would slow his progress, but he'd never return to his former emaciated state. Every millimetre of fat and muscle on his body was another wasted week.

David stared out through the murky safety plastic of the window to the vast expanses of woodland outside. It was all dead and grey at that time of year. Still, he stared out at it, out into the fog and twisted wild as if it were something more captivating than miles of decay. I stood beside him to watch the trees sway awkwardly in the wind, their branches and leaves flaking off like dry skin.

"How have you been since we last spoke?" I asked.

David turned to me. "Don't."

"What?"

"You're talking as if we're two people capable of having a pleasant conversation, but I don't know you, you don't know me, and the only reason we're in the same room together is because I've asked you to kill me. I don't have the energy for this."

"How would you like me to talk to you?"

"I don't know, just don't expect me to respond."

His irritability was understandable – he was hungry and frustrated. If I had been in his situation I would have prised my fingernails off with a sharpened toothbrush weeks before just for something to do. That being said, he should have been used to isolation and monotony if his diaries were anything to go by.

David hobbled back to the bed, and as conversation was at a standstill I decided to sit with him in hope that the close proximity might instigate some form of dialogue. I felt immediately uncomfortable – I have never enjoyed the unfamiliarity of familiarity. By the look on his face David wasn't entirely keen on it either.

"Trent will be here soon," I said, trying to figure out a topic that might be of interest to him. "When he arrives a phys aid will come to help you down to the visitation room."

"Okay," he replied.

"I'll be there, but I'll be outside. It'll just be you and him in the room… unless you want me to come in with you, of course."

"Not really."

"How about one of the psych aids? Or a phys aid?"

"I don't need anyone."

I smiled. No amount of bluntness could stop my questioning; I had much more stamina than he had.

"Trent is your friend?"

"Sort of."

"How long have you known him?"

"Few years, I think."

"How did you meet?"

"Can't remember."

"Come on, surely you can remember something like that?"

He thought for a moment. "He did some work in my building. Then he started helping me out and getting me food and things when I... when I couldn't anymore."

A deep shame gradually revealed itself in his face. I hadn't seen that expression on him before.

"Was he your carer?"

He made a noise that was a mixture between a snort and a tut. "No, of course not, he didn't wipe my arse or anything if that's what you're thinking. He just got me stuff. Groceries, that sort of thing."

"Are you close?"

"Not especially."

Feeling a sudden resistance to the subject, I changed tack.

"Have any of the psych aids explained what happens during a visitation?"

"Only every day for the past week. Over and over and over again. And then once again this morning just to make sure."

"Would you explain it to me? I'd like to know what you know."

Sighing, David fell backwards onto the bed, raising his thin, sinewy arms above his head to stretch. "It's hardly a difficult concept. It's an observed visit. You watch us talk and then pull the plug on it if we say anything you don't like. What more is there to say about it?"

His top had risen slightly. I could see a pulse throbbing beneath the blotchy skin of his abdomen. I quickly turned away, trying to hold back a shudder.

"It's not about stopping you from saying something we don't like," I said."We just need to protect you from things that might compromise your treatment."

"Yes, I know. They've been through it all with me a hundred thousand times. I know what's going to happen."

“I just want to make sure you know that this isn’t like visiting someone in a hospital. And it’s definitely not like visiting someone in a prison.” I let that sink in for a moment.”We have to prepare you mentally for this and record everything that’s said in order to protect you, your visitor and the facility. You have a right to have visitors, of course, but you’ve entrusted us with your care. We’ll do whatever is necessary to help you.”

I waited for him to say something. He didn’t so much as look at me, so I added, “There’s still time to invite more people to visit you. You can invite absolutely anyone. You could call friends, family members… even your parents.”

He tugged at the bottom of his top, mercifully concealing his flesh. “Well, my parents and I don’t get on, so I don’t think that’s going to happen.”

“What about friends?”

“I don’t really have any.”

“So why choose Trent? Why do you want him to visit?”

He went very still. “I don’t know really, I suppose I just need to see a familiar face before I go. Someone who isn’t a part of this place.”

The lies came quickly, but they weren’t executed particularly well.

“That’s not the reason you asked for him.”

“Isn’t it?”

“Am I supposed to believe you invited a man who occasionally bought you groceries to visit you at a relief centre, just so you can see a familiar face? That doesn’t make sense to me. And why would he accept? There’ve been countless reports of relatives being attacked in their homes for supporting relief patients, so why would he put himself at risk just to see an acquaintance? He’s had to go through several inspections and security checks, will be paying astronomical travel fees to get here and will have the potential burden of being the last person to visit you before your relief. Does that not seem a bit much to you?"

"What do you want me to say, then? I don't see why you bother asking any questions if you're just going to disagree with the answers. Why don't you just tell me what to say and I'll say it?"

"We both know you're not being honest."

"Do we?"

"I might not know everything about you, David, but I know when I'm being lied to. I'm just trying to do my job. You're going to need to open up if you want us to help. There's still a very real possibility that your treatment will be discontinued."

"Well, you try opening up about your personal life with that thing staring at you all day long."

David pointed at one of the cameras on the ceiling. As he sat up it moved with him. He stood and walked from one side of the room to the other, all the while the camera followed him vigilantly.

"The cameras bother you?"

He stopped pacing and lent on the bed, his cheeks inflating and deflating as he tried to recuperate from the sudden bout of exercise. "Of course they do. That kind of thing would put anyone on edge, don't you think? They're watching me while I sleep, eat and shit. It's constant."

"They're there for your safety."

"I don't feel very safe."

It was the perfect opportunity to gain his trust. I slipped the e-Noter out of my pocket, tapped into the camera settings for the room and paused the activity on each machine.

“They’re on a timer. You’ve got five minutes.”

David watched as each camera swivelled downwards to face the floor.

“Are you serious?” he asked. “They’re off?”

I nodded.

David walked up to each machine – well, the machines he was aware of – and waved his hand in front of its lens. Once he was satisfied, he smirked and stumbled back to the bed, his weak, spindly legs shaking with the effort of holding up his meagre weight.

“They’re all off,” I said, “so you can tell me why Trent is coming to visit you.”

His smile faded. “Why? Why do you need to know about him?”

“Why won’t you tell me?”

“Because it doesn’t just affect me, does it? Everything I say about him will affect him as well.”

I shrugged. “The cameras are off, so none of this will be on record. I can’t relay anything you say to the committee without evidence. I just want to know.”

David shot another few glances at the cameras. There was a twitch at the side of his mouth and he ran his hand through his hair a couple of times, causing the smoothed ends to spring outwards.

“I was telling the truth,” he said quietly. “He ran errands for me, mostly over the last few months before I came here, but he... he’s helped me out a lot more than that.”

“What does that mean? You were friends?”

“No, I wouldn’t quite put it like that.”

"Then how would you put it?"

"I hired his services."

"What do you mean? What did he do for you?"

David lowered his gaze and picked at the threads that were sprouting from a seam on his trouser leg. He snapped a couple off and dropped them from a height, watching them float gently to the floor.

"He knows why I'm here. He helped me."

"I don't understand. You're VDA. You volunteered to be here."

He remained silent, pulling harder at the strands of cotton.

"Why are you here then, David?"

"I need to be here."

"But why did you volunteer?"

"You know why."

"From the sounds of it, I don't think I do."

"He must have told you."

"Who?"

"He did. I can tell. He told you what I did. You wouldn't look at me like that if you didn't already know."

The cameras slowly whirred back to life, all shifting simultaneously to focus on David. He twisted round to look at them, his shoulders stiffening instinctively.

"So that's that," he said.

"Can you just…" I began, but the phys aid knocked on the door to announce Trent's arrival.

# 17

David was bent forward, one hand on the wall and the other on his knee as he gulped oxygen back into his lungs.

"Try to breathe," one of the phys aids suggested.

After a few raspy breaths he managed to respond with a derisively raised eyebrow, but his eyes were wide with panic and a red tinge clouded the white of his sclera.

"Your respiratory difficulties are the result of malnutrition," I explained."You'll be able to walk longer distances once you've put on a bit more weight."

"Shall I get him a wheelchair?" the phys aid asked.

"No. I'll walk," David said sharply, attempting to straighten up.

I wish I could have told him the truth. It was futile trying to hold onto dignity, pride or whatever it was he thought he had, because in the end no one can stop themselves from dribbling and defecating in death. The concept of dying with dignity was even disassociated from modern day euthanasia because it was thought to be nothing more than a social construct, and relief is the only medically attainable result. I've always wanted so desperately for my patients to see this, but it's illegal to try and influence them in any matter other than their medical wellbeing. Instead I had to watch as they foolishly clung on to the remainder of their modesty, and the stronger they held on the faster it left them – like grains of sand falling through their fingers.

Despite the delay, we arrived early at the visitation room. I call it a room, but it was technically two adjoining rooms separated by one-way glass. One side was set up like a standard viewing gallery, with rows of hard chairs. The other had sofas, carpeted flooring and a coffee table, autumnally decorated in oranges, red and browns. It was supposed to feel inviting without being overly stimulating, but I always found something unsettling about it. It was windowless and smelled strongly of artificial scent. It was a stage room with contrived warmth.

"How are you feeling now?" I asked, helping him to sit.

"Shit." His whole body was shaking. The changes to his diet had affected him far more than I had initially calculated.

I turned to a young phys aid – she couldn't have been older than eighteen, the faint remnants of acne still simmering beneath her skin – and ordered David a two hundred and thirty-seven millilitre carton of Pertita, the orange supplement drink commonly used at the time. The second it arrived David tore the corner off the box, tipped the contents down his throat and winced as the thick, gloopy liquid slid down his gullet.

I tried not to think about how quickly he had just downed five hundred calories. In minutes he had consumed hours, if not days, of my time.

"Trent will be here in a moment," I said, sitting on the sofa opposite him. "I'm just going to go through a few things about the visit first, if that's all right with you?"

It seemed to take a lot of effort for him to nod in response.

"As you know, the visit will be monitored and recorded. Right now Trent is talking to your psych aid about what he can and can't say to you, so keep in mind that he might not be able to respond to everything you say. Boar House requests that you avoid discussing our patients and staff as a general rule, and only discuss the details of your treatment if you feel comfortable in doing so. Some suggested topics include fond memories, people you both know, hobbies and shared interests. You may discuss current affairs, but if we feel the topic will affect your progress we will be forced to interrupt the conversation. We allow a maximum of two interruptions before we terminate the visit.

"Physical contact is permitted but sexual contact is not. You must remain seated throughout the visit but if you need anything or if there's an emergency, there's an alarm beneath the coffee table. Can you see it?"

"Mmhmm."

By the time I had finished talking the supplement had kicked in, and David looked a lot more comfortable – although his fingers drummed the seat of the chair incessantly.

"Is there anything you want to ask me?" I asked.

"Can I have another drink?"

"I'll ask the psych aid to get you some water. Anything else?"

He thought for a moment. "Nope."

"You sure? You seem nervous."

"I'm fine."

"You can cancel this at any point, you know, it's not too late."

"I'm fine."

"So you're happy for Trent to come in now?"

"Yes, fine, I'm fine. Just bring him in."

His hand trembled slightly as he pushed the hair out of his face. But that could have been the remnants of hypoglycaemia.

I left the room just as the lead psych aid was bringing Trent down the corridor. He looked younger than I had imagined, with a face that was too attractive to be considered ugly but too unpleasant to be appealing. He had rich chestnut-coloured eyes that were distractingly close together, a bulbous nose with extraordinarily smooth skin and an almost non-existent upper lip framed by a strong, square jaw. He had all of the right features but they didn't sit right together, as if he were disfigured in some way but I couldn't tell what was amiss.

He grabbed my hand and shook it roughly while I introduced myself.

"Pleased to meet you," he said.

He spoke slowly and deliberately, and I immediately felt defensive. He knew who I was. He must have researched me.

"I'll be speaking with you afterwards," I said, ensuring my tone was void of question. I needed to make it clear that I wasn't asking for his permission; technically, visitors to government-run facilities require authorisation to both enter and leave the premises. To put it simply, as soon as civilians enter Boar House they are effectively relinquishing their freedom. I could have held Trent for days, perhaps weeks without explanation if I had wanted to, but Watts was too cautious of media backlash to allow that. Still, I planned to question him for at least a few hours.

He clasped my hand again and squeezed it.

"I look forward to it."

* * *

I sat down in the viewing gallery just as conversation began between Trent and David.

"Is everything okay?" Trent asked. He leaned back and brushed dirt absentmindedly from his trousers.

"Yeah," David replied, reclining on the sofa but failing to mirror Trent's composed stillness. "You?"

"Yeah."

David smiled nervously, then seemed to notice the cameras and large one-way mirror beside him. He forced his expression to flatten.

"Is it all sorted?" David whispered. He must have known I could hear every word from the viewing gallery.

"Yeah," Trent replied at a normal volume, "you don't need to worry about anything."

"Are you sure?"

"Yes, I'm sure. I told you before, David, you can rely on me."

"How's mum and dad doing?"

"They're fine. I haven't spoken to them myself, but I know they're fine."

"Okay, that's good."

"They went to see them."

David leant forward. "Really? What happened?"

"Don't worry, it went well. He wasn't there."

David chest deflated with relief. "And how is…"

Trent's face darkened. "Don't ask me," he said sharply, "you know not to ask me."

"Come on, really? Does any of that matter now?"

"Yes, it does. It really does."

"Just tell me, please. I need to know if everything's okay between us."

"*No*. It's not worth it. Anyway, I don't know anything. Just be happy that everything's going well for you."

What followed was the longest, tensest bout of enforced silence I have ever witnessed. Both men stared into the mid-distance, occasionally tapping a foot or scratching an arm as time became engorged and sluggish. I'm not usually one to feel uncomfortable in the face of awkwardness, but the deliberate nature of this social vacuum was hard to ignore, like a high-pitched noise or an unreachable itch. I found myself closing my eyes to break away from the suffocating atmosphere.

Finally, nearing the end of the hour, Trent broke the quiet. "It'll be over soon."

"Yeah, I know." David sighed.

"Keep your head up."

"I'm trying. It's boring as hell in here."

Trent shrugged.

"Do you think my parents would come if I asked them to? At the end?"

Trent looked around as if there might be someone else to take the question for him. "I'm not sure that's a good idea, you don't want to put them through something like that. Not after everything."

David looked away, struggling to maintain his composure. For the most part he succeeded, but he seemed to quiver a little under the strain of it.

A gentle female voice spoke over the tannoy: "You have five minutes left of your visitation. Please remain in your seats until you are escorted from the room by a member of staff."

Nothing more was said between them. No goodbyes, no hugs, not so much as a look of acknowledgement. David stared at the floor while Trent studied the ceiling until the psych aid came into the room, helped David to his feet and took him away.

Ten minutes later, I was sitting in front of Trent, adrenaline brewing uncomfortably in the pit of my stomach as I handed over my e-Noter for him to sign. He appeared calm and smiled knowingly.

"This is just to confirm who you are and what's going on," I said. "You don't need to sign it if you don't want to, it's just protocol, but I am legally allowed to keep you here under the Visitation Act for as long as I see fit. Take your time to go through and understand the information. If you have any questions, just ask."

"It's fine," he said, scribbling on the screen and handing it back.

I had hoped his face would betray him, that I would catch a glimpse of weakness brought on by the formal nature of the e-Noter, but no such luck. He wasn't just calm, he was defiantly serene.

"So," I said, interlocking my fingers, "how do you know David?"

"I don't know him at all really, didn't know him before he came here and certainly don't now. I met him on a job and we got chatting. I live near him and helped him out with a few things."

"Why?"

"Why what?"

"Why did you help him?

"Have you seen him? He's a state. He needed someone to help him."

"Well yes, I believe he's been in need of help for some time, but you didn't need to be that person. Why didn't you call the authorities? The council?"

"All I did was get him groceries, that's all. He asked me to."

"You got him food?"

"Just a few odd bits, fruit and things."

"Did you see him eat any of it?"

"No. I was never with him for very long."

"But if you wanted to be there to help him out, to be a good Samaritan for your fellow man, surely your concern would have extended to his weight? It's hard not to notice how emaciated he is."

"Yeah, but I didn't know whether he was ill or something. I didn't like to ask. Like I said, I don't know him that well and we didn't say much more than a hello. We discussed the weather, that's about as deep as it got."

"Really? So why were you talking to him about his parents?"

Trent smirked. "I don't know what you're getting at."

"Come on now, Mr Williams, if you want to leave here quickly you need to be honest with me. You know I can keep you here for as long as I want to. Why were you talking about them?"

"Not that it's any of your business, but he asked me to make sure they're okay before he came in here."

"Why did he ask you to do that?"

"Because I was the only one to ask. Things were left in a weird place between them, apparently. They didn't get on."

"Why?"

"I don't know, he never told me. He just asked me to make sure they're okay."

"How did you do that?"

"I know their neighbour. He keeps an eye on them."

"And how did you know I'd visited them?"

"The neighbour told me."

He had already exhausted me. I could tell if I pushed too much he would feign ignorance – he was far too confident to buckle under pressure – but if I tried to appeal to reason or sentimentality he would dismiss it immediately. Burying my frustration seemed like an impossible task, but I needed to wear him down by keeping my tone even and my questions at a consistent pace.

"Earlier on David asked you about someone," I said."Who was it?"

"His parents."

"No, after that, there was another person he wanted to talk about. You said, 'Don't ask me, you know not to ask me'."

"Oh right," he nodded, poorly mimicking a look of sudden realisation, "that would be Valerie."

"Valerie Harmon?"

"That's her. One of the last things he said to me before he came in here was that he liked her, but they stopped talking a while back. He wanted to get in touch but I told him it was a bad idea. It would upset her."

"But you said conversation didn't go much deeper than the weather. Are you saying they're together?"

"No, never have been, but he's madly in love with her."

*Bullshit.* Trent's face said it all – he clearly expected me to go along with it all, as if I would believe David's sole reason for relief was rejection.

I felt an almost uncontainable rage build within me – did he really think I was that stupid? That I wouldn't look into every detail?

But that's always the way, isn't it? It doesn't matter if anyone believes the lie so long as there's sufficient audacity to go through with it. Trent was helping David to cover up his true motive for relief because there was something in it for him. But why? How?

I swallowed to try and get rid of the tightness and bitterness in my throat. "So," I said slowly, "let me get this straight. David is in love with Valerie."

"So I've been told."

"What did he tell you about her?"

"They met at school and hung out a bit. Were friends of friends, that sort of thing. I don't think Valerie ever took any notice of him. A few years ago he asked if he could use her parents' house to focus on a work project. He told her it was too noisy at his flat or something. But it was all a lie and he'd spend the day in her room looking through her stuff until her younger brother got home. He'd then ask the brother all sorts of questions about her and leave before anyone else got back. She found out after a few months and took his key back, so I'm guessing that's why he decided to come here. Because she rejected him and thought he was a creep."

It was utter nonsense. There was not enough shame in David for that to be the true reason. If he was a lonely, obsessive pervert he would have been defensive, particularly when I mentioned his sexual preferences, but there was nothing like that in him. If he *had* stalked her he certainly didn't think it was wrong, and it wouldn't have been the push he needed to apply for Boar House.

I had to look down at the auto-transcript to take a break from Trent's infuriating expression, but when I looked back up his knowing smirk was still there. If anything, it had deepened further into the corners of his mouth.

"Earlier David asked if 'it's all done'," I said, "what did he mean by that?"

"Ah yeah, his funeral arrangements."

"You're involved in his funeral arrangements?"

"He asked me to make sure he was cremated, which I've done. I just had to send off some documents to his local council. You can check it if you like."

"I will. But tell me, why did he trust you with that sort of thing? After all, you're just a man who bought him groceries and chatted to him about the weather. You may have also kept an eye on his parents and heard him talk about the love of his life, but you're nothing more than a regular nice guy, right?"

"I don't know what to tell you." He sighed, fidgeting to get comfortable on the sofa. "Can I have a glass of water? It's stuffy in here."

"In a moment," I said, acknowledging the drips of sweat running down own my back. My mouth felt as though it was filled with thick, wet clay. "Why did you tell him I had visited his parents? And how did it, as you put it, go 'well' because his father wasn't there?"

"He didn't want his parents to be bothered by you lot. He knew you'd investigate him but, as you know, the visit was short and sweet. His dad is apparently a right piece of work and makes his mother's life miserable. Look, this is going to be a really boring talk, okay? I know nothing. I don't know why I'm even visiting the guy, I just got sucked into this whole thing. If I knew it was going to be this much trouble I wouldn't have bothered."

"Have you ever visited a patient in a facility like this before?"

"You know I have."

"Nine. You've seen nine patients. Why?"

"My uncle died in a facility surrounded by his family, but there are loads of people who don't have that. They do it alone. I understand a little about what they're going through and I meet lots of people on the job who need someone to talk to. I just get roped into these things and I haven't the heart to say no."

"You don't seem like a charitable type of person."

"Well, you don't seem like the kind of person who would have a job caring for human beings, but who am I to judge?"

My head was throbbing. "Look, Trent, you say you hardly know David yet you arranged his funeral. It's obvious you're covering something up for him."

"Really? Like what?"

I ignored his challenge. "Did you know David made video diaries?"

Trent gave a genuine smile this time. "I don't know anything about that, whatever he did in his own time is his own business. I just bought him groceries. Can we break for some water yet?"

I ignored him again. "Tell me about yourself."

"Why?"

"Because I want to get to know you."

"Why don't you just look at the file you have on me?"

"Because it doesn't say anything interesting."

"I'm a boring guy."

"I just don't believe that. Why would you visit him? Why would you help him?"

"I felt sorry for him."

"Really?" I leant forward until my chest was almost resting on my thighs, the volume of my voice boomed loudly, now completely out of my control. "He told me. You know something. You know why he's here."

"He's here because he's wants to die."

"He hired you."

"News to me."

A burst of energy coursed through me. I stood and booted the underneath of the coffee table, which cracked and tumbled across the floor. I felt the nail on my big toe split and a warm wetness seep across the top of my sock. Trent barely even flinched.

"Just tell me!" I said, the adrenaline now flooding my vision."Why is he here? What did he do?"

"I can only tell you what I know."

"So *tell me*."

"Just take a minute to chill out, yeah?" he said, the grin now gone, but I could hear him trying to suppress a murmuring of laughter from escaping his chest. "He has no friends, okay? And he might as well have no family – he screwed things up with them but I don't know what he did, all I know is that they want nothing more to do with him. He's a lonely guy with few prospects. He's not very confident, he's stupid, sad and scared and I think being here is the best thing for him. There's no going back for people like him."

That term silenced me for a moment. "'People like him'?"

The smile returned and he shrugged. "Hopeless cases."

"He said you know what he did. He hired you. You know why he's in here."

"He's in here because he's been a creep to Valerie and she doesn't want him. His family doesn't want him. He doesn't want himself. What more is there to say?"

"There's plenty more to say."

"He paid me a bit of money to sort some things out for him, that's all."

My texter vibrated. It was an emergency meeting request from Logue. As soon as I saw his name flashing on the screen my anger grew cold, as if his hopelessness had somehow managed to transfer through the device and into my consciousness.

"I have one final question," I said, trying not to pay attention to the fact that the inside of my shoe had become sodden and tacky, "why are you here?"

"Same reason as you," he replied.

"And that is?"

"To make sure David gets what he needs."

# 18

"What do you want, Logue?"

I didn't go to sit with him and he didn't stand to join me. Our conversation was held across three rows of seats in a randomly chosen viewing gallery, further accentuating the vast space between us. When he looked down and took a deep breath I let myself fall onto the nearest chair, knowing the meeting was going to last longer than my body could handle.

"Now the visitation is over," he said, leaning onto his knees, "and you've got everything you need. When are you going to meet with the committee?"

"But I haven't got everything I need. I've got a lot of loose ends to deal with first."

"Nieve, please stop dragging this out. We need to get this done."

"You mean *I* need to get this done."

"He's ready now."

"He's not – he hasn't reached his target weight for a start. Plus I need to interview the cleaners and set up another meeting with the WORMs. Trent didn't give me anything to work with, so I'm no closer than I was a few days ago. Why the sudden urgency, anyway? What's this about?"

"You know what this is about. I need to get this fucking over with."

There was a creeping threat in his tone that I'd never heard before. It made the hairs on my arms stand up, as if the room was charged with static electricity. Words were suddenly completely unattainable to me, and all I could do was sit there and allow the blood to race around my body while I waited for something to happen. He rung his hands together and I felt the muscles in my legs tense, readying me to move if I needed to.

I knew he was facing me, I could feel it, but for the first time I found it impossible to look back at him. It wasn't his simmering viciousness that frightened me but his completely uncharacteristic behaviour. I thought I had seen every side of him. I suddenly wanted to go to my cottage. I wanted familiarity.

"You have to listen," he said softly, rocking slightly. His feigned calmness left me cold. "He's only a few pounds away from his target, I'm sure they'll accept that. You can book a meeting with Watts tomorrow and get an appointment with the committee by the end of the week. The procedure could be over within a fortnight."

He was breathing heavily. Even with the distance I could smell his staleness. I wanted to move but I had the feeling he would follow me if I tried.

"You know I can't do that." My voice sounded far away.

"We need to stop prolonging the inevitable."

"What do you want?"

"I could ask you the same question."

"Me? I have no agenda other than to help our patient."

"We both know that's a lie."

I finally looked up at him. His forehead had a sheen of sweat and he was blinking nervously.

"You know what's going to happen to me, don't you?" he said.

I nodded. He must have been at the final stage of his imminent retirement: acceptance.

"We need to stop prolonging the inevitable," he said again.

"I'm not holding onto the case on purpose here. I need to do things properly. You may be at the end of your career but I'm at the start of mine, and if I screw things up now I'll have to live with it for the rest of my life."

"If you want to do things properly, why are you starving him?"

I pinched my inner left thigh hard to stop myself from reacting.

"I don't know or really care what you're doing," he said, wiping his face with his sleeve, "but I know your type. You're in over your head with something, probably trying to prove everyone wrong." He scrutinised my expression, and although I tried to relax my facial muscles I must have given something away. "I knew it! You're using him for something, aren't you? Don't worry, I honestly don't care what you're doing, I just need this to be over."

"I can't do that."

"Like you said, you have your whole career ahead of you. There'll be plenty more Davids."

"You don't get it."

"No, *you* don't get it. I don't care how you do it, I just need him to get to committee. It's over now, he's the last one, I just want it to stop."

I swallowed the metallic taste that had coated my tongue and inner cheeks. "I'm not rushing a case just because you want to retire," I told him. "Why don't you just leave? Watts has been begging you to go for months. I know he'll keep you on the books until your retirement fund comes through. You won't lose out on anything."

He gave a disbelieving snort. "Are you genuinely stupid or just fucking with me?" He examined my expression again, searching my eyes for clues. "You really think that's what's going on here, don't you? Jesus. They all think you're really smart, you know that? But you're not. You're a parrot. You're not even a person, you're just pretending to be. I've always thought there was something off about you. It's like you were made in a factory somewhere. The generation of acceptance, that's what Watts calls people your age, but none of you actually feel anything. You don't even know what's going on around you. You think you're doing something decent here but you have no idea. You have no idea what the world is like."

"Why don't you explain it to me then?"

He chuckled and shook his head.

"You're really pathetic, you know that?"

"Yes, I know." He looked weary as he said it. "The stupid thing is, I fought for all this. I made this happen. I made *you* happen. I thought the end result would always stay the same, even if the reason behind it didn't."

He paused.

"Then Miller Park happened."

I was sick of the hidden meanings. The politics. I was sick of no one saying what they meant and the looks they all gave me for not understanding their unspoken intentions. If I knew why people did that, if I understood how to play the game, I'd discover the reason why David was lying to me. I'd know why Logue was so determined to screw up his life. It was a language that everyone else could speak, and although I didn't want to think like them I had to in order to understand them.

It took everything I had just to say the words, but the answer would be the beginning of things for me. I could catch up, no longer the strange and distant anomaly I had been all my life.

"What happened at Miller Park?" I asked.

"What?"

"Tell me." I swallowed. "Please."

His glasses fell down his nose a little, his lips parting in surprise. "You don't know? You seriously don't know?"

He wasn't ridiculing me, but I didn't know how to answer him.

"Things will get better for you when the case ends," he said. "When the case ends I can go. Things will be better for you. Trust me."

He left, and I felt like a passerby watching everything unfold with no context, no translation. His words a never-ending echo.

The humming in my pocket was like an undercurrent to the buzzing in my brain. My hands, numb and heavy, fumbled in my pocket to extract my texter.

*WORMS at gates.*

Everything snapped back into focus.

## 19

The first time I watched someone die I remember feeling quite indifferent.

Despite its mysterious, frightening and almost mythical reputation, the death itself had little impact on its surroundings. I was waiting for something to hit me, something to shock, disturb or inspire me. An impression would surely be left from an event instinctively feared and loathed by every creature on the planet.

Nothing.

I had been prepped by my teachers for a devastating onslaught of grief intermingled with confusion, fear and disgust... but not apathy. It wasn't in any way strenuous to cope with apathy, which ironically made it even more burdensome.

I kept telling myself that someone had died. A person had just died. In front of me a heart had stopped beating, a brain had stopped thinking. The leathery, damaged exterior may not have looked as though it had belonged to a person, but inside it had been a living breathing human, someone who had feared and loved and ultimately expired mere inches from me. Perhaps it hadn't sunk in, perhaps I couldn't digest the enormity of what I had witnessed.

Maybe I hadn't concentrated enough the first time round. The second time I endeavoured to focus solely on the procedure itself, noting what to check, when to wait, what to watch for and when to act, honing in on every step of the process to see if I had missed something that would trigger the emotional repercussions I was told to expect.

But I had read all of the textbooks. I had studied each step so closely that it was like watching a projection of my own mind, and concentrating on each element didn't manage to bring about any form of emotive response.

It was strange how dull it became, how monotonous. Not only was I numbed to it, but as the patients had been guided through the procedure so many times they also seemed uninterested in their own death – nodding at odd intervals, eyes glazing over to stare at the ceiling or the bed sheets, fingers drumming in slight impatience. The apprehension of such a natural occurrence had been stripped away, leaving them resigned and submissive, displaying only a feeling of mild unpleasantness akin to waiting in a long post office queue.

But David wasn't like that. David wasn't awaiting for the inevitable. There was more than death filling his everyday thoughts, and his layers of secrecy had reinforced my obsession with desistance to such an intensity that death was similarly the last thing on my mind. Was I the only one who saw uncertainty in his eyes where acceptance should've been? Did that make me all-seeing, or was I delusional?

The follow-up visit from the WORMs didn't do much to answer that vital question. Marvin was pissed at me and Lane didn't even bother to show up now that their reputation was in tatters. Word had got round that an inexperienced euthanasist had found something they hadn't, so they were no longer considered the best of the best. With icy professionalism, Marvin spent hours going through the case again with me, this time with the addition of photographs showing David's demolished ceiling and a chemical dissection of the swabs taken from the resulting mess. I didn't hear anything I hadn't heard before, until Marvin curtly informed me that Grays Hill Cleaning Company had changed name and owner and we were subsequently no longer permitted to investigate them. I have always both respected and despised legal loopholes.

Desperation sunk its sharp teeth into me once again and I reacted irrationally. I began pulling David out of his room at all hours of the day and night. If a question or theory popped into my head I would book the nearest assessment room and ask him outright for answers, no technique or strategy in mind as I did so. He was passive and robotic, unless of course I happened to mention Valerie.

"Tell me about her."

"Her name is Valerie Harmon. She's my age. I knew her at school. She hates me."

"Why?"

"You know why. She thinks I'm a pervert."

"Are you?"

Silence. He always refused to so much as acknowledge that question, let alone answer it.

"Were you friends at school?"

"Not really. To her I was just…there."

"What were her family like?"

"I never met her parents, only her brother."

"Tell me about him. How did you meet Daniel Harmon?"

“He’s nice,” he said. I could tell there was genuine affection there. “He always asked me if I could help him with homework. He wanted me and Valerie to get married so I could hang out with him all the time. He planned everything, but she fucking ruined it all.”

Now that the anger had tinged his words there was no point in asking any more questions. He’d start to flinch at her name, and the only sentence that would leave his month was, “Can I go back to my room?”

He’d ask that over and over and over until I relented.

It took a hurried comment from one of the aids for me to get my act together. A forty-something psych aid named Leanne took it upon herself to mention one of my unscheduled visits in David’s notes, but luckily I found it before anyone else had seen it and deleted it. I removed her from the case as well, but it made me realise there was a real need for structure and consistency in my assessments.

I set up the Gumfrey drawing test, which despite my initial reservations gave surprisingly significant results. I told David to draw an abstract image of what he believed represented his future, and he spent a total of seventy-five seconds scribbling away. On the screen he revealed a thick, black circle with crosshatched lines in grey and dark brownish red in its centre. I didn’t need to wait for the picture to come back from analysis to get a gist of what it meant. From my rudimentary sketch analysis classes I could tell the bold, black circle represented a certainty, or a single and unique goal, and the crosshatched lines revealed hidden doubts and concealments. I could see a blend of aggression and nervousness within the frenzied strokes. When looking at it from afar the picture was bold and certain, but with closer inspection it was impatient, self-protective and manic.

The next assessment I arranged was the Unsolvable Puzzle, designed by J.N. Sørensen. The puzzle was a series of twisted metal spirals that could be taken apart and put together again quite easily, but a mechanism within it clicked into place when a particular piece was removed. A magnet was required to slot the mechanism back so the rest of it would fit. For a depressive or suicidal person this could cause a number of heightened emotions, including anger, frustration, despair, self-loathing or apathy, but David worked on it for around an hour. He exhibited frustration every now and then, but for the most part channelled his energy into trying to solve it. Eventually I had to take the thing off him and told him he had run out of time, again to gauge his reaction to failure. I also refused to reveal how the puzzle could be solved, and he argued with me at first before accepting the situation, admitting it would add nothing to his life to know how to put it back together.

The results for both of these tests revealed behaviour not indicative of desistance. My satisfaction at reinforcing my theory was once again harboured by apprehension – it was becoming increasingly likely that he'd fail at committee.

My final assessment was the most consequential. The Estevez test, which is no longer used, involved sitting the patient in a dimly lit room in front of a screen that displayed a random selection of positive and negative words, phrases and descriptions. The patient's heart rate, eye movement and sweat levels were recorded and analysed, and a brief interview was conducted in-between each phase of the assessment to evaluate the emotional state. The patient was asked at the end of each interview if they would like to stop the test, but were told if they did the assessment would resume again the next day. This was not true. The Estevez test was only performed once with each patient.

There were ten phases in all. In the first phase, which took just five minutes, David had a minor reaction to three positive words: smile, cute, love. This caused a mildly elevated heart rate and an increase in eye movement. The only negative word he had an above average reaction to was 'creep'.

"How did you find the first phase of the assessment?" I asked as the lights came back on.

"Fine."

"Out of ten, how would you rate your feelings of happiness?"

"Five."

"How would you rate your feelings of sadness?"

"Five."

"How would you rate your feelings of anger?"

"Five."

"Are you okay to continue to the next phase of the assessment? We can postpone it until tomorrow if you'd like."

"No, I'm fine."

The lights dimmed again and the projector added subject pronouns.

*I am annoying.*

*I am happy.*

*I am loved.*

*I am important.*

*I am hated.*

The charts revealed a reaction to the words ‘useless’, ‘nothing’, ‘wrong’ and ‘gross’, but he had no reaction to any of the positive words. I asked the same pointless questions as before and David gave the same pointless answers.

Two more phases gave similar results to the first two. However, in the fifth phase the screen showed an amalgamation of the words David had reacted to most in the previous phases. He began to twist and writhe in his seat, his discomfort beginning to brew.

*You are cute.*

*You are creepy.*

*You are useless.*

*You are wrong.*

*You are gross.*

*You are pathetic.*

By the eighth phase David was trembling and sweating profusely.

*DAVID IS CREEPY.*

*DAVID IS PERVERTED.*

*DAVID IS DISGUSTING.*

“Turn it off, just turn it off!” David stood suddenly, ripping the various tubes and suckers from his face, underarms and chest. He managed to cut his arm in the panic and blood spattered onto his clothes.

There were many phys aids and psych aids on standby in the room, but I was the first to reach him. I grabbed hold of an antiseptic cloth and pressed it to the cut on his arm while somehow managing to persuade him to sit back down on his chair. A psych aid turned the projection off and switched the lights on before fussing around me. I snapped at her to get back.

The floor was dotted with thick droplets of blood, as was the front of my uniform. David was looking around at it all, his eyes darting from one crimson spot to the next as he sucked in short gasps of air. I peeled back the antiseptic cloth to check on the wound, which was small and had already stopped bleeding, but I allowed one of the phys aids to check him over anyway. The brief medical examination seemed to calm him down quite a bit.

"I'll take him back to his room," the phys aid said, leaning forward to lift David up by the armpit.

"Not yet," I said. "We haven't finished the assessment."

The psych aid held onto David, trying to get him to stand. "I really should take him back."

"After the interview."

"But…"

"We need to conclude the test or this will have all been for nothing, won't it? Do you not understand that?"

The team looked at one another, then at David, who had pushed the psych aid away and was now sitting quietly and looking at the floor. His skin was more flushed than usual, but other than that he seemed fine.

"How did you find the eighth phase of the assessment?" I asked him.

"Fine," he said, although there was a slight quiver in his voice.

"Rate your feelings of happiness out of ten."

"Five."

"Sadness?"

"Five."

"Anger?"

“Five.”

“Are you okay to continue to the next phase of the assessment?”

“Yes”

“Are you sure? Do you have any questions?”

“Yes, I’m sure. And no, I don’t.”

I looked back to the psych aid. “Well, you heard him.”

I indicated for the team to step aside as I set up the equipment again. David drew back as I reattached the suckers and tubes to his body, but he didn’t ask me to stop.

He battled through the next two phases with an expression of immense pain on his face. By the time the lights had come on and I had asked my final round of questions, he was quietly crying.

Was he depressed? Maybe. Was he scared? Definitely. But David wasn’t anymore suicidal than I was. There was still life in him.

# 20

I woke with my head slumped forward. As I straightened up a hot, searing pain erupted at my shoulders and spread down to my lower back. Gritting my teeth, I lifted up my arms and heard a series of clicks and cracks.

David chatted mindlessly on the screen in front of me. I must have been asleep quite a while – his hair was long again and had started to cover his eyes. I bent forward and switched the machine off. It was three o'clock in the afternoon.

Watts had left several messages on my texter requesting an emergency meeting. I assumed it was about my progress with David since that was the only thing the man ever wanted to hear about. According to his schedule he was in his office for the next couple of hours, so I gathered my things and left the Hub.

His door was wide open as I approached, which was odd. I could hear him halfway down the corridor, pacing up and down the length of his office, bickering bitterly with someone on the phone. The closer I got, the more unfamiliar the scene appeared: his suit jacket was crumpled and strewn over his chair, his tie loosened and his shirt untucked with large, grey sweat patches soaking through at the armpits and the small of the back.

I decided to wait by the door.

"I'm telling you, we have neither the beds nor the manpower to cope with that right now. Yes, I'm very aware of that. It doesn't look great, but what am I supposed to do? I can't move them, not without causing a fucking commotion upstairs. I know. Yes. No. Why? What do you expect…" And then he saw me, his damp face glinting in the light, his nostrils flaring like a rhinoceros ready to charge. "Oh, Hindeman. Sit down, will you? I just need to check… Yes, Jay, okay I'm on it, just don't go crazy if we can't handle all of them. Most of it will do, yes, but I'm not sure what timeframe we have here. June? Are you serious? Fine. I said *fine*, what else can I say? Anyway, I'll call you back, Jay. I'm speaking with her now. Yes, I know, that's why I have to go. She's in my office. She's here right now. Okay? Okay. Yeah, bye. Bye."

I stared at the bars on the outside of the windows, hoping to appear lost in thought so Watts wouldn't think I was interested in his conversation. I felt as if I had walked in on him undressed, and it felt distasteful.

He sat behind his desk and attempted unsuccessfully to smooth down his hair. He looked exhausted. Not tired, with the dark rings under the eyes and the slightly dazed expression that everyone gets from time to time, but the kind of exhaustion that emanates from the skin, posture and odour. It was obvious through every aspect of his physicality.

"Where have you been, Hindeman?" His authoritative tone had been softened by fatigue.

"I was in the Hub working on the case."

"I've been trying to contact you for hours."

"I'm sorry, it's just been a bit intense and I lost track of time. Is there anything in particular you wanted me to update you on?"

"No. I don't give a shit about any of that. I want to know why you've been pulling the aids back from the case."

"I was…"

"You're wasting time, that's what you're doing. You don't need to be doing their job as well as your own, they're quite capable of performing a few simple tests while you get on with the case. I've looked into it, Hindeman, and you've catalogued a hell of a lot of hours without actually producing anything. I suppose your dedication is quite commendable, but you've done enough. We need to start progressing to the relief procedure within the next week."

"Did he tell you all this?"

"Who?"

"What did he say to you?"

"If you're referring to Logue, this has nothing to do with him. I haven't heard from him in days, weeks maybe. For god's sake, just do your job before you lose it. There's nothing physiologically wrong with the patient, is there?"

"No, but there's still so many video diaries left that could give us the answers we need."

"As far as I can see, there are no more questions that need answering."

"But the videos, Valerie Harmon, his parents, the cleaners, it's all…"

"Irrelevant."

"He's not even reached a healthy weight yet. The committee won't accept him."

He groaned and rubbed his eyes until they became red and puffy."How long will it take to get him healthy?"

"Three weeks, maybe four." That was a lie, of course. He could get there in a few days if I pushed him hard enough and he drank a few glasses of water before the weigh-in, but I was going to hold on to that time with everything I had.

"You have two. Two weeks. If he doesn't have an appointment by then you're off the case and Logue will be his sole euthanasist." He thought for a second. "Or I'll bring someone else in. Either way you have two weeks. Get this done."

"If I just had a bit more time – three weeks, I could do this properly with three weeks."

"No."

"Then I need to take twenty-four hours' leave. I need to use a MediTaxi."

"No. I won't give you that time. I *can't* give you that time. Not out of the facility's own pocket."

I tried to take some deep breaths but it didn't stop the hot panicky feeling from spreading through me.

"Just a day," I said. "Just one day, that's all. I just need to see his parents and Valerie Harmon, that's all."

"His parents? What for? I've already given you time for them, what more could you need? And who is this Valerie anyway?"

"I've got some new information that I need to discuss with his parents. As for Valerie, she may be the reason David admitted himself to Boar House."

Watts shook his head at every single word, causing my fear to curdle into anger.

"Ignoring the facts will only cause more trouble for the facility," I said flatly. "If that got out, god knows what that would mean for the future of Boar House."

His eyes snapped up from the e-Noter on his desk.

"Are you threatening me?"

"No, sir. Just stating facts."

"Because if you were I would kick you out of this facility so fucking fast..."

"I'm simply voicing my concerns. Just imagine what would happen if the committee found out so many elements of the case had not been properly investigated."

"What kind of things?"

"There's a lot that doesn't match up, but I have some theories that I think could help clarify the parts that don't make sense."

"Theories? What theories?"

"I'm working on something that could help patients like David. It could mean big things for Boar House."

"This isn't the time to start making a name for yourself, Nieve. After a couple of years of getting your head down and working hard people will listen to you, I'm sure of it, but right now you could ruin us all. Don't you understand that? You would be out of a job and everything would come crashing down around us. These are very, very sensitive times."

"My theory has nothing to do with ego, I swear to you. It will eradicate doubt in the profession…if I could just prove it with David first."

"He's a cert for relief though, isn't he? We can't have another failed case. Not now. We really need to get this one through."

I quickly ran through the wording in my head. “He’s a definite candidate for relief. I just need more time.”

“But I have no time to give you, if I grant you leave this late in the case it will look like we have serious doubts, don’t you see? I can’t let you go. The shit with the WORMs has already got people talking.”

“What if I took it out of the time owed to me? My personal time?” Watts immediately leant forward to refuse my offer, but I raised my hand to stop him. “I can say my mother died.”

“Is she actually dead?”

“My biological mother is. She’s been dead for decades, but her records aren’t connected to mine in any way so no one can find out about her. I’ve never had a birth certificate and my records only go back to the age of five, when I was put into foster care. None of it contains details of my family. If anyone asks, although I doubt anyone will, I can tell them my mother got in contact with me a few years ago through a private detective. No one will investigate it, why would they? *How* could they?”

I could feel my heart fluttering madly in my chest as he slowly began to nod. “It might work. Even you would take time off for your mother’s funeral.”

I didn’t reply. I just pushed my e-Noter towards him with the leave request form open and waited for him to sign.

## 21

The receptionist with fake hair must have been at the tail end of her night shift. Her eyes scanned me lazily as I approached the desk.

"Documents." She held out her hand. I gave her my e-Noter, which she returned almost immediately with a pass. "Just to remind you, the facility is not liable for anything that happens outside of the grounds. Our insurance only extends to the end of the drive, so if you have any issues out there you should contact the police. Your driver has insurance, but only for the vehicle. Sharing confidential information with anyone while you're out is a criminal offence. Do you have any civilian money?"

"I don't need it."

"You'll need food and water. The cafeteria isn't open yet."

I patted the bag draped over my shoulder. "I have enough with me."

A sigh burst from her slightly parted lips. "You should've got money. Well, as there isn't any petty cash left I suppose you'll have to do without. You can go now."

I nodded a thanks – I was grateful the process had taken less than five minutes – and left through the main doors.

As I walked down the steps a handful of protesters shouted out some of the usual chants and slogans, but the crowd wasn't particularly animated at half past five in the morning. In spite of their lethargy it was clear their numbers had grown, perhaps even doubled since I had first met with the WORMs. By midday I wouldn't have been surprised if that number doubled again.

The MediTaxi I had hired was the only vehicle on the drive. It cost just under two and a half month's wages but I had full use of it for the next twelve hours. I knocked on the window and presented my pass to the morbidly obese driver sitting behind the wheel, but she didn't make any indication as to whether she had acknowledged it or not. I climbed in the back anyway and told her his address, and she replied by starting the engine. We drove through the front gates and onto the road in silence – the protesters didn't bother trying to stop us.

For around five miles we zigzagged down narrow potholed roads that wormed through a thick maze of trees, braking intermittently to allow farming vehicles, horses and people on foot to pass. I had to close my eyes to stave off the motion sickness. Eventually the ground smoothed and stretched out as we drove past villages, from which point the view on either side became an endless sea of swollen, grassy banks. I got bored of the sight of it pretty quickly. Patients often babbled on about the beautiful view leading up to the facility, but to me it was like staring at the same patterned wallpaper for hours on end.

Twenty minutes later we were forced to pull up at our first check-in. Before the MediTaxi had even come to a complete stop the travel officer had thrust his hand into the driver side window and grappled for the vehicle identity card. The driver grunted at the fingers waving wildly in her face and slapped the card into them.

I rolled down my window with my travel pass in hand and the officer turned towards me with an odd smile that only showed his startlingly white upper teeth. Their colour must have been the result of an expensive chemical treatment that was popular at the time. They looked unnatural and disgusting; the thought of his chalky incisors gnashing down onto food made me feel ill.

"Got your ID?" he asked, even though I was clearly offering it to him.

Rather than simply scanning the pass he began to read it, and within seconds his teeth slid beneath his lip and his thin, scraggly eyebrows seemed to jump up into his frown lines. When he had finished he nodded sagely, scanned the pass and handed it back.

"You're from that Boar House."

"Yes."

"What are you doing out and about? Bit dangerous for you to be roaming the countryside, even with your guard dog."

No sooner had the words left his mouth than the driver threw open the door and stepped out of the MediTaxi. She was a big woman – incredibly tall as well as broad – and the officer instinctively placed his hand on his weapon.

But the fat woman just smiled, her short, frizzy ponytail blowing softly in the breeze like a bunch of cotton plants. She nodded at his weapon. "No need to panic, sir, I was just thinking that if you're going to spend some time chatting to the passenger I might as well get out and stretch my legs."

The officer looked the woman up and down and, realising there was nothing he could do with such a mass of a person other than shoot her, nodded for her to get into the vehicle and went back to his station. As she pulled away she smiled briefly at him, then looked at me through the rear view mirror. "Next time only give them your pass if they ask for it. It'll be a lot easier, trust me."

I heeded her advice, and for the rest of the journey not a single travel officer asked to see my pass. The car was checked six more times, but never its occupants.

Over time the grassy green hills flattened, became ploughed and turned into concreted streets, towns and housing estates. Once we had passed some ornamental parks and turned left at a large fountain decorated with chipped cherubs and leaping fish, the driver announced, "We're here," and pulled onto a gravel driveway.

Valerie lived in a tall, thin, elegant white building. There were pink rose bushes on each balcony and a few larger ones planted in neat little rows along the front garden. It was vastly different from the area David had lived in, mainly because it looked loved. There were benches and beautiful old-fashioned lampposts placed along the street, the pavement was wide and uncracked and there was no litter left to dance about in the breeze. I would never have thought that a pleasant-looking home could have the ability to instigate joy in me, but as I looked at it through the MediTaxi window I felt serene. It felt easy to be in that space.

"Come on, love, I don't have all day." The driver shifted in her seat, causing the whole vehicle to rock from side to side. "In or out? Should I go on my break?"

"Yes," I said, stepping out of the car. "We have to leave in an hour to go to the next location, but I'll be at least thirty minutes."

The second I shut the door she reversed out onto the road with a screech that made my eardrums feel as though they'd been scratched. I hated the clash of sound and scene.

I strode up the path to a door that was light cream in colour. To the left hung a list of names and numbers handwritten in cursive within a thick wooden frame. A silver door phone sat snugly underneath. Valerie's name was in the middle of the list, coupled with the number 505, which I typed carefully onto the keypad. The ringing went on for quite a while before it was interrupted by a muffled click.

"Hello?" came a high-pitched voice trough the speaker.

"Is that Valerie Harmon?"

"Yes, it is, who's this?"

"My name is Nieve Hindeman, I work for the Boar House Relief Centre."

There was a pause. "Okay. So…what do you want?"

"Just to speak to you. It'll only take a moment, I promise."

She sighed heavily and the front door unlocked with a click. I pushed it open before she had a chance to change her mind.

The heady scent of powdery, artificial flowers followed me from the lobby into the lift and remained with me all the way up to the fifth floor. Apartment 505 was at the end of the corridor and was the only door to have an ornate silver knocker nailed to it. I lifted it and allowed it to fall out of my fingers to make a sharp tap sound. Moments later the door was eased open and a small, elfin face appeared in the crack.

"You can't stay long," she said. She stared at me for a few seconds before reluctantly stepping aside to let me in.

The living room smelled sweet, like milky vanilla. With soft, natural lighting complimented by a spongy, peach-coloured carpet, I immediately felt the urge to kickoff my shoes and recline on the comfortable-looking sofa wedged into the corner. The room made me feel delicate, as if I were a woman from the eighteenth century who would faint at the slightest shock or bout of physical exertion. The room wanted to me to lie down and sink into its softness.

But Valerie didn't want me in there. She ushered me into an airy, white kitchen and we sat at opposite ends of the breakfast table, both waiting for the other to speak. With each second that passed, she shrunk further down into her chair–and she was already tiny, with delicate wrists and matchstick legs. Her diminutive frame was accentuated by wide eyes and straggly auburn hair that frayed out at the ends. I might have been jealous of her doll-like features if her complexion wasn't smothered in acne scars, dark red spots and smudged, orange freckles. Her protruding bottom lip also made her look like a spoiled, loathsome child.

"What do you want?" she said, giving in first. Her voice was inelegant and piercing, and didn't sit right with the gentle aesthetics of her apartment.

I felt more at home than she looked. Her tiny hands kept flitting between smoothing down her frizzy locks to tugging at the waist of her cheap, high-necked dress. I quickly realised she was pregnant, but her efforts to conceal it only made it more obvious. I looked away out of politeness.

"Can I record our conversation?" I asked. She shrugged, which I took to be a sign of concurrence. "As I said outside, my name is Nieve Hindeman and I'm from Boar House. I'm working on David Myre's case."

Valerie's only response was to pull her dress over her bump.

"Could you tell me what you know about David? I assume you already know he's in Boar House."

"I don't…yes, I heard about it."

"Do you know why he wants relief?"

"I don't care."

"Well, I came mainly to ask about your relationship with David."

"We don't have one."

I nodded. I assumed I'd get some resistance. "I just need to know what you know about him. Is that okay?"

A tear formed in her left eye. As she nodded it came loose and ran down her face.

"How did you meet David?"

"School."

"Were you friends?"

"No."

"Friends of friends?"

"As far as I know, he didn't have any friends. He'd just attach himself to people and follow them round for a bit until they managed to get rid of him."

"But he used to go to your house quite regularly, back when you lived with your parents and your brother."

Valerie looked down at her lap. "We've never been close."

"So why did he come to your house?"

"He was in love with me."

"But that doesn't explain why you would allow him to stay at your house while you were out."

She gulped audibly. "He asked."

"What did he ask?"

"I really don't know him at all. I mean…" She paused, looking as though she were trying to recount something. "He said he had to work on something. I said yes because it was easier than saying no. I hardly knew him. I *don't* know him."

"I just want to make sure I understand what you're saying. You don't know him well but you know he was in love with you, and you let him go to your house to work on something while you were out because it was…easier?"

She nodded, somehow reassured by my summary. "He needed somewhere to go and knew my house was empty, so I let him go there for a while because if I said no he'd just keep on asking me. But it got weird, he was looking through my stuff. I told him he scuffed the wall in the hallway and couldn't come round anymore. I said if my parents found out they'd kill him. They would have killed him."

The sudden severity of her words took me aback. Her family seemed to be a particularly sensitive subject.

"I hear he got on well with your brother?"

She clutched her face as though I had slapped her. "He didn't. Look, I don't know anything, all right? I don't even know him. I know nothing about him." She pushed her chair back and stood up slowly, her hand shaking as she pointed to the door. "You're going to have to go now. Please go."

"Why do you keep saying that?"

"What?"

"You keep saying you don't know him."

"But I don't know him. I didn't know him well before and I don't know him at all now."

"His mother said exactly the same thing to me, over and over. Has someone been talking to you?"

"I don't…no one, I don't know what you mean."

She began to tug furiously at her dress, her movements getting faster and faster. She took a couple of steps back and yelped as the heel of her foot collided with a cupboard.

"Did Trent tell you what to say? Is he behind this?"

"I don't know who that is."

"Is this even your apartment?"

"Y-yes, of course it is."

"I've read up about you. You're a clerk, clerks don't live like this. How long have you lived here?"

"Six months."

"And before that?"

"I lived with my parents and brother."

"Are they nearby?"

"You can't speak to them!" she shrieked. "Leave them alone, don't even go near them! I'll…I'll…you know what? I'll call the police. If you go anywhere near them, I'll call the police. My family will tell me if you ever go there, and then I'll call the police."

She was panting and clutching her bump. Angry tears dripped from her chin onto her collarbone.

My chair scraped against the tiled floor as I pushed back with my feet. I stood and took a couple of steps towards her, feeling like a giant in comparison. "A man's life is at stake here. You know that, right?"

"That's on him. You can't blame anyone else for that. Now get out before I call the police."

"Is it David's?"

"What?"

"The baby."

Valerie looked down with a puzzled expression, as if she hadn't realised it was there, and then touched her stomach gently with her fingertips. Her gaze gradually met mine again and, after a long, deep intake of breath, her head went back and her mouth flew open.

She laughed.

It was a horrid, hysterical screech. There was no control over the ear-piercing cry that she seemed to rip out of her own throat, and as her jaw widened and the sound intensified I could see brown lumps of food wedged in between the gaps of her teeth. I couldn't look at it, wanted her to stop, wanted to grab her face to make that awful shriek end.

It must have been over in seconds, but the noise went on and on and on in my head.

"No, it's not his," she said, so quietly it was almost a whisper. "I'd have scraped out my insides with a knife if he had touched me. I'd have torn everything out if the thought even crossed his mind. But I'm not his type. Thank god, I'm not his type."

I couldn't breathe, I was swirling.

"What did he do?"

She didn't answer, just picked up the phone and pressed it to her ear. She ended the call to the police mid-sentence as I shut the door to her apartment.

# 22

I wanted to go home.

Part of me wished no one would answer, but the door was opened almost immediately by a broad-shouldered man with a moustache and thick, dark brown hair. I knew at once he was David's father.

"Good afternoon, Mr Myre." I extended my hand. "My name is Nieve Hindeman. I'm from Boar House."

As he opened his mouth to speak, Mrs Myre scuttled out of nowhere and shoved him aside, placing one hand on his chest and the other in front of my face.

"I think you need to go," she said to me.

Mr Myre stepped forward and pushed up against her, mostly to show there wasn't a chance in hell of her being able to stop him. He had the almost complete opposite build to David.

"I want to hear what she has to say," he said, not taking his eyes off me.

Mrs Myre began shaking her head. "I don't think…"

"I want to hear what she has to say," he repeated, his voice low. "Get in. Both of you."

I looked back to my driver parked on the curb. I'm not sure what I was hoping for, perhaps some sense of support, but she was already fast asleep with her head tipped back, her tongue lolling out of her mouth like a dog's.

When inside I was directed to the same armchair I had sat in before, with my back to the window. Only this time Mr Myre was the one sitting in front of me. His wife stood with her back against the wall. She looked close to tears.

I began the recording.

"So?" Mr Myre gestured for me to speak.

I fumbled through my notes, trying to remember exactly what I wanted to get out of this meeting. Everything had flown out of my head – all I could think about was Valerie and that hysterical, screeching laughter.

I ran my tongue along my teeth, trying to get some moisture to circulate around my rapidly drying mouth. "As you both know, I'm in charge of David's treatment at Boar House. I've come across a lot of new information recently and have quite a few questions I think you both might be able to help me with. I'd also like to address a few points I don't think we fully covered last time."

"Last time?" Mr Myre shot a glance at his wife.

"Mick, I…"

"What did you tell them?"

"Nothing, I promise, she just asked what David was like. When he was a boy."

He turned to me, pupils dilated into predatory slits. "Then why are you back here? I don't know anything about him, didn't before and certainly don't now. Shouldn't you be asking *him* why he wants to be in there?"

I nodded. "We are, Mr Myre, but I'm afraid he's not being entirely honest with us."

He snorted. "Nothing new there. You know, we don't have to be honest with you either. We have rights. More rights than he has."

He relished his anger, enjoyed the revulsion he had been given the opportunity to express. With each word he seemed to get lighter, his mouth less taut and his eyes clearer.

"I promise, once I've asked you my questions I'll go. I'll be as quick as I can."

"Fine. But we don't have to answer. I know my rights and I know we don't have to answer."

I nodded again, trying to remain still in case he mistook my impatient fidgeting for nervousness.

"My first question is about his apartment," I said. "Why did you pay for David to have it professionally cleaned before he left for Boar House?"

He looked at his wife briefly, and her palpable fear seemed to bring him strength. "We were the ones who put the deposit on that shit hole so he didn't have to live with us. If we hadn't hired cleaners we would've never seen that money again."

He lied just as poorly as his son did, but I didn't challenge him. I couldn't.

"Why didn't you want him living with you?"

"We had a falling out."

"What about?"

"He's lazy. He manipulated his mother. He lied time and time again. He made our lives hell."

"How did he do that?"

He smacked his lips reproachfully. "If you bothered to get to know him you'd find out for yourself pretty quickly. He doesn't appreciate anything or anyone, and takes whatever he can, whenever he can. He's got a real sense of entitlement, you know? Just thinks the world owes him. When the world tells him no, he lashes out."

"What did he do?"

Mr Myre shrugged.

"There must have been something, something big that made you feel like this. No one cuts all ties with their son for no reason."

He began running his fingers through his hair, and for a moment all I could see was David.

He sighed, his expression darkening. "Have you got family?"

"Yes," I said, and was immediately stricken by how easily the lie had slipped from my mouth. "Actually no, I don't. I don't know why I said that."

"What happened to them?"

"I was put into foster care when I was very young. Never knew my parents. I was never in the same place for very long."

As predicted Mr and Mrs Myre were quite stunned by my honestly. The silence became weighted, and while Mrs Myre wrapped her arms around herself, as if cold, her husband looked through me, clearly unhappy within his thoughts. "In some ways you're lucky," he said."You'll never know what it feels like to have your unconditional love destroyed. I hate David for making me go through that. He made me feel something only a monster should feel."

"Tell me what he did," I begged, unashamed at how shrill and desperate I sounded, not that he cared. He glanced in the direction of the front door, no doubt imagining me leaving.

It was not going to end there.

"He had an old school friend. Valerie Harmon."

Mr Myre stiffened, his knuckles protruding as his thick hands balled into fists.

"You need to leave now," he said, standing up.

"She's the reason David went into Boar House, isn't she? What did he do to her?"

"Nothing," he spat. "Just leave it alone."

"What did he do to her when he went to her house?"

"Stop it."

"Did he have a relationship with her?"

"I said stop it."

"Do you really want me to stop? If you don't tell me what's going on I won't be able to help him. I'll have to let him go, which is something I don't think you want. It's definitely not something I want. He might be put in a psychiatric hospital for a few weeks but they'll let him out eventually, and then the journalists will swarm in as they always do. They keep tabs on our failed patients, did you know that? It's all on public record. They scour it looking for stories. His file may be confidential, but I won't hesitate to tell the press everything if you don't help me."

Mr Myre snatched my e-Noter from the coffee table and hurled it against the wall. The loud crack of plastic forced a deep coldness to pump through my body, urging me to run, but I didn't give in to it.

"Whatever he did, he'll do it again. And the parents always get the blame. He'll do it again and everyone will know that it was *you* that let him do it."

There was no time to react. He lunged and wrapped his fingers around one of my wrists, yanking me forward with such force that I fell facedown onto the carpet, narrowly missing the sharp edge of the coffee table. He proceeded to pull me across the room, with the left side of my face dragging and burning against the carpet, his wife all the while screeching for him to stop.

As he rounded the corner to the hallway he misjudged the flexibility of my body and simultaneously bent my arm back while smacking my face into the wall. I cried out and he dropped my hand for a moment, but he soon picked it back up and continued to lug me toward the front door.

I must have passed out, because the next thing I knew I was laying outside with my shattered e-Noter on the path next to me. The slam of the front door jumpstarted me to consciousness, and although I was reluctant to get up I forced myself to grab the larger pieces of my e-Noter and stumbled toward the MediTaxi. The lightest breeze stung the burnt flesh on my face, but I was pretty sure nothing was broken – although my arm was becoming increasingly stiff and sore.

I fumbled trying to open the vehicle door, which soon woke the driver, and eased myself onto the back seat.

We drove for at least five minutes before the MediTaxi screeched to a halt.

"What the hell happened?" she said, her small pink mouth rounded with genuine concern in the rear view mirror.

"Just drive back," I said.

"I need to call a doctor."

"No. It's superficial. Take me back, I'll deal with it myself."

"I can't do that."

"Take me back."

"We have to call the police. Who did this? Was it the people in the house?"

"No."

With my clear refusal to cooperate she had no choice but to start the engine again. However, before she pulled away I saw a thought cross her mind, like a passing shadow momentarily darkening her expression. She hesitated at first, but then couldn't help herself but ask.

"Did you deserve it?"

I thought about it for a second. "Probably."

# 23

Disembodied palms slapped and smeared every inch of the windows. I shut my eyes to the chaos.

It took twenty-seven minutes to get through the crowd and onto the drive. When the engine was finally switched off I didn't move, but sat motionless hoping my body would stop throbbing and my mind would settle. The driver turned around in her seat – or as far round as she was able to given her considerable size.

"You need to tell someone," she said.

"Why?" I asked, brushing reddish brown flakes from my lap.

"I don't know, you just need to tell the people you work for. They need to call the police."

"It doesn't work like that."

"How does it work, then?"

I leaned back into the seat, grimacing as the skinless patch on my arm brushed against the vehicle door. "If I tell the police the case will be halted."

"People shouldn't be able to hurt other people and get away with it."

"That's such an infantile view to take. It's natural for people to hurt one another. In fact, it's a vital component of existence. Anyway, I'm not seeking retribution here, if anything I'm more concerned about why it happened."

"What *did* happen?"

“I mentioned someone. A name.”

The driver’s brow crinkled in thought. “Someone attacked you for saying someone’s name?”

“More or less.”

“Sounds to me like you hit a nerve.”

She had meant to come across as facetious, but she was right. By tapping a sensitive subject I had inadvertently performed a psychological reflex test.

I hid my face as I got out of the car and scuttled around the facility building to the cottages. Once the door was closed behind me I stood naked in front of my full-length mirror to evaluate the severity of my injuries. Some of it looked worse than I had expected, particularly the damage to the front of my legs, but I didn’t need stitches and felt able to deal with it myself. I began by cutting the flapping skin from my knees, shins and forearms with nail scissors, then cleaned the wounds and covered the worst areas with bandages. My face looked less dramatic after I had washed the blood from it – it just looked and felt as though it had been sunburnt, although I did have a visible bump on my forehead and the beginning of a black eye. I placed an ice pack on it and downed several painkillers.

I was lying on the bed wearing nothing but a cold flannel on my face when there was a knock at the door. I pulled my robe on without thinking and came very close to screaming; the coarse fabric felt like serrated knives scraping against my skin.

By the time I was able to get to the door Logue had begun to walk away. He stumbled back on himself, gasping at the sight of my face. He didn’t exactly look great himself, with bags under his eyes so swollen they looked like bruised bottom lips.

“Jesus, what the hell happened to you?” He looked down to my robe and took a few steps back. “I’ll come back later.”

“What do you want, Logue?”

He checked over his shoulder to make sure we were alone. “I had a meeting with Watts this morning, while you were on leave. He told me to take the case to the committee if you don’t do it soon.”

My heart began to race, pumping hot blood through my body that felt like acid beneath my skin. I opened the door a little wider and pulled him inside, immediately revolted by the sight of his scruffy, crumpled body in my clean home. I had to bite my tongue when he lowered himself on the end of my bed.

“So,” I said, “what did he say?”

“We need to stop prolonging…”

“…the inevitable, I get it.”

“Nieve, what the hell happened to your face?”

“It’s nothing.”

“Who did that to you?”

I saw no harm in telling him. “David’s father.”

He wasn’t in the least bit shocked. Watts must have told him about my visit. “Did you call the police?”

“No, and I won’t.”

“Why not?”

“Because, like you’ve said a million times, we need to stop prolonging the inevitable. David is not viable for relief.”

Logue shook his head, slowly at first and then with gathering speed, his body rocking slightly with the effort of it. “No. No, no, no, no... What are you saying? Why are you doing this?”

"I told you from the beginning that this case didn't feel right, and after today I know for sure. All I need to do is get the truth out of David and I'll bring my findings to Watts by the end of the week. The case will have to close, of course, but it won't be the disaster everyone's expecting it to be. In fact, I think it might be the best thing to happen to Boar House."

"You can't do that. The evidence is solid. You'll be thrown out of here in seconds. Do you really want that? To be unemployable for the rest of your life?"

I took an old e-Noter from my desk and logged in. Despite the violent death of my newer one the recordings had still automatically uploaded to my account. I played him the meeting with Valerie.

*"He didn't. Look, I don't know anything, all right? I don't even know him. I know nothing about him. You're going to have to go now. Please go."*

*"Why do you keep saying that?"*

*"What?"*

*"You keep saying you don't know him."*

*"But I don't know him. I didn't know him well before and I don't know him at all now."*

*"His mother said exactly the same thing to me, over and over. Has someone been talking to you?"*

*"I don't…no one, I don't know what you mean."*

I stopped it to find the next file.

"Now listen to his mother," I said, "this a few weeks ago, the first time I met her."

I clicked play.

*"I feel like I've never had a son. I know nothing about him. I didn't know him well before and I don't know him at all now."*

I searched again. “Now his father. This was from today.”

*“I don’t know anything about him, didn’t before and certainly don’t now.”*

“And now Trent from his visit to the facility.”

*“...didn’t know him before he came here and certainly don’t now.”*

I handed the e-Noter to Logue, but he just watched the blank screen.

“It’s incredible,” I said, unable to hold down my excitement any longer, “they’ve all used the exact same phrasing. Exactly the same, every single one of them. This is huge, isn’t it? They’ve all been told what to say. They’re all in on it, for whatever reason, they all want David dead. And David wants to be dead too...well, he does, but not really. I think he’s been forced into this but won’t say anything and I don’t know why. I don’t know what they have over him, but it’s something big. And then there’s the cover up with the cleaners and the money... god, this is big, but the biggest part is yet to come. Just one more week and it’ll be perfect.”

“You sound fucking crazy,” he said coldly, although I detected a slight tremble in his voice. He switched the e-Noter on again.

*“But I don’t know him. I didn’t know him well before and I don’t know him at all now.”*

*“His mother said exactly the same thing to me, over and over. Has someone been talking to you?”*

Logue gave a derisive chuckle. “You sound paranoid there. Actually, you know what? It sounds like you’re threatening her, frightening a vulnerable pregnant woman into saying stuff she knows nothing about.”

I snatched the device back. "Oh, come off it. She's saying the same things David's mother did when I first met her. The phrasing, the way she speaks, it's identical. Whoever prepped Mrs Myre prepped Valerie too, you can hear it."

Logue cocked his head to one side and gave me a look of such exaggerated pity I thought I was going to scream. "Nieve," he said, sighing, "you're seeing things that aren't there. You've been doing this since the beginning of this case. I know you want there to be more to it than there is, but all you're doing is frightening a load of people who shouldn't even be involved in the case. I warned you before to just look at the patient and gather evidence from him, but instead you're going round and round with your conspiracy theories. You're a good euthanasist, you don't need to do all this to prove yourself."

"Conspiracy theories? What's wrong with you?"

"VDA patients are the most difficult to deal with and it's easy to be consumed with doubt, but I know you're better than this. Maybe Watts is right. Maybe you should take a step back for a little while and let me finish things. You can have another go at a VDA case in a few months from now, when I'm gone and you've had a chance to collect your thoughts. You've been working yourself to the ground."

I laughed in sheer disbelief. "You're fucking insane. One minute you're doing nothing for him, the next you're trying to hurry him through the system. What exactly are you trying to do?"

"Oh, so now I have an ulterior motive too? Is everyone in on this conspiracy?"

"It certainly looks that way."

He got up and began to hover near the door. He looked so jittery I half expected him to make a break for it."Watts is getting impatient," he said, putting his hands in his pockets and then on his hips before allowing them to hang awkwardly at his sides. "You obviously don't understand how crazy things are right now but believe me, if you take any more risks with the case he'll fire you and you'll be out on the streets, no career or retirement to look forward to, no money, no hope, *nothing*. You might think of me as a worthless sack of shit but at least I know where I'm heading.

"You've got to play the game to get anywhere, so just let this one go already and move on. Think of your future, because if you ruin things now you're ruined for life, don't you see?"

Yes. I could see it. I could see through his wild desperation, and the truth made me feel like I was on fire. But I couldn't move. I just had to stand still and let myself burn.

"You fucked everything up on purpose," I said through gritted teeth.

All those failed patients locked up in institutions for life. All that time wasted. All those people left to suffer so Watts would panic and push Logue into early retirement. Logue had taken his time, probably for the sake of realism as well as to guarantee himself the highest retirement settlement possible, but now I was involved he wanted to hurry things up before it went too far.

For a moment he almost tried to argue, but the look on my face must have told him to give up. "Everyone does it," he said, "and I've given my life to this place. For years I did a job that no one else wants. I did the dirty work and made things easier for everyone but myself, but now I want something to live for."

"So you can live with yourself now you've ruined people's lives for a good pension plan?"

"Their lives were already ruined."

"I suppose you've had to lie to yourself a lot recently, why stop now?"

"I mean it, we're not helping anyone here. We're just getting rid of them. Being a euthanasist doesn't mean what it used to."

"Stop trying to justify what you've done. This is the most important job there is. We're providing relief to desperate people who are either facing a miserable death or a miserable life. We're doing what people for centuries have wanted to do but didn't have the guts to. We're the closest there is to curing the incurable and giving the ultimate pain relief. We end suffering."

"Suffering is essential."

He began to ring his hands, which were slender and bony with thick, coarse hairs sprouting unevenly across the back. They were untrustworthy, cruel hands, like a chimp's; intelligent and capable, but quite inhuman. They looked familiar, I understood their shape and the way they moved, but they were completely unlike my own.

Questions and thoughts and realisations were exploding in my brain, hampering me from knowing what to do next. I desperately wanted to fix what he had done.

Then I realised, the past may have been muddied and spoiled, but the future was still waiting. There was still a chance that the past might not catch up with it.

"I've been recording everything," I blurted out.

He shook his head, sighing. “Nieve, I know you haven’t,” he said flatly.”Why would you?”

“Every word you’ve said will be given to Watts tomorrow morning. I have it all.”

Lies are only convincing if they’re believed by the teller, so I imagined twelve microphones hidden in various places in and around the cottage. As I spoke I glanced at two of them placed near the door. “I knew something was wrong so I prepared myself. This isn’t the only place I’ve rigged either, I’m not stupid.”

He shook his head again but turned to face the spot I had just looked at. “Even if you had all the evidence in the world, Watts still wouldn’t listen to you. He’d throw you out. He wouldn’t risk it.”

“You’re probably right,” I said, “which is why I’m going to threaten to go public. I’m willing to sacrifice myself for that end. No one else should get away with what you’ve done.”

His face drained of pinkness, leaving a greeny grey tint to the skin. “You’ll be shut down, everything will be. If you’re thinking of the patients’ welfare you should know that this is just the thing the government needs to close us down. Euthanasia will be made illegal again.”

“If that’s what’s needed to make things right, then I won’t stop it. I can’t let you leave this unscathed, Logue, I couldn’t live with myself if I did.”

“You don’t know the half of what goes on. I did what I had to.”

And then he was on top of me, first grabbing at my stinging arms and then squeezing my throat, which pulled the burnt skin of my face taut. A guttural yell was pushed out of me as salty tears spilled from my eyes and burnt my torn cheeks.

"No one will listen to you," he said, squeezing harder.

I rammed two of my knuckles hard into his temple. He scrambled off me, clutching the side of his face, so I took the opportunity to stand up and gain some leverage. I only realised my robe had untied when he looked up at me with a mixture of embarrassment and fear.

I prepared myself for a secondary attack, but there was none. He just slowly stood up and tottered uneasily toward the door.

"I'm sorry," he mumbled, gripping onto the door handle to keep himself upright.

"No you're not," I said, but he didn't hear me. He had already left.

# 24

At three twenty-five the next morning I was fighting my way out of a foggy, painkiller-induced sleep. I had to get to the dementia ward.

That's where my career at Boar House had started. For the first seven weeks as a newly qualified euthanasist I was assigned to night shifts on the dementia ward, which was where most young euthanasists started. It was some sort of endurance test cooked up by the senior staff; there were a high number of dementia patients with non-existent sleeping patterns, so it was an incredibly active ward at night.

I was introduced to it as the 'cat circuit' because the patients were like wailing strays, batting and scratching whoever got too close to them for no apparent reason. My evenings there were spent rushing from bed to bed administering medication, helping phys aids strap bodies to tables and checking vitals. Finding an ND (Natural Death) was every euthanasist's worst nightmare, so we searched for them with a paranoid frenzy.

The dementia patients never stayed for very long. Those aged seventy-five or older were usually processed within a week, yet despite the quick turnaround I found the time I spent with them to be overwhelming. With each lap of the cat circuit I wanted to end it. End the waiting, the simpering, the slow agonising nothingness, their fear and their slack mouths.

I began dreaming of slitting the wrinkled throats of every yowling creature I met, but in my subconscious the skin was thick and leathery and I'd have to dig and stab and rip with my nails to get to the fragile cords inside. I would then snap them with my hands and feel immediate satisfaction. Sometimes they wouldn't die straight away and would gurgle and splutter while the blood spilled out from their torn necks. They weren't aware of it though, and would continue to flounder brainlessly like newborn babies until they eventually stopped moving altogether.

What disgusted me most about them was their smell of sour milk and urine, which never seemed to leave me no matter how roughly I scrubbed myself after each shift. For a while I mistakenly believed it was what death truly smelled like – I had only experienced the chemical stench of sterilised refrigerators in the morgue, but in time I realised it wasn't death I smelt. It was cruelty. That vinegary ammonia was what prisoners of war, hostages and third world hospitals secreted. It was failure, horror, suffering, panic. Only the living can rot and stagnate in such a grotesque way.

The violence in my dreams soon bled into my working life. I began gripping the patients' arms far too tightly, and if I were ever left alone with one I'd cover its mouth with my hand to shut it up. I couldn't stand their loud squalling, but my fury was never satiated because they would simply continue to babble once my hand was removed. I overdosed a few of the noisier ones to get them to sleep for longer periods of time, but the fear of being found out soon stopped that.

After five weeks of doing my nightly rounds I asked a senior colleague how they were able to stand it. They candidly replied, “I just remind myself that it used to be much worse.” I looked into it, and it’s true. Retirement homes were once paused moments in time, in which nurses waited for infirm bodies to disintegrate. They would allow patients to decay for years without doing a single thing to help them, and sometimes the families prolonged the suffering with stabilising medication and painful forced feeding. Protesters may call relief facilities death houses, but the alternative was sheer torture.

Retirement homes were bad, but the respite hospices were beyond evil. With further research I discovered terminal cases used to be shoved into joyless hovels, all fully aware that they’d never leave again. Eerie and cheerless halls would be crammed with the young and the old, all drugged to the point of losing complete control of their bodies. The idea has always made me feel claustrophobic.

It’s the wait that really gets to me. How could they stand the wait?

After those initial seven weeks on the cat circuit I was finally given my own cases, which somehow helped me develop a tolerance to the slow suffering of the elderly. I think it was the weight of responsibility that centralised my thoughts, forcing me to focus on the long-term.

For years after I worked steadily without even the slightest suggestion of instability, but my tolerance had slowly started to disintegrate from meeting David. Hatred was seeping its way back into my brain and I was becoming erratic, taking risks – perhaps not the sort of risks Logue and Watts thought I was taking, but I was growing careless all the same. I couldn't understand why it was happening. What had changed?

And then it was three twenty-five in the morning and I knew I had to get to the dementia ward. If I went back to the beginning, perhaps whatever I had lost would click back into place. Perhaps I'd be able to understand what had triggered the change within me. Perhaps I'd be able to get the furious whirling in my brain to stop.

My brain was a thick, muddy pool and my body moved as though it was trying to wade through it. I was simultaneously hypersensitive and numbed, feeling pain but not quite sure where it was coming from, but I ignored the protests from my inflamed skin and pulled on my uniform. As I flung open the door and began running past the cottages it all blurred into a dull, fizzing ache and I was able to move quite quickly.

The facility was cold and dark at that time in the morning. During nightshifts the lights in the corridors only switched on when they sensed movement, so it was like I had a spotlight illuminating the way. Some of the other euthanasists complained about the dangers of this energy-saving lighting as they were unable to see what was coming up ahead, but I found it reassuring. It blocked out everything but the immediate.

As my spotlight and I rounded the corner it immediately disappeared into a haemorrhage of light coming from an open interview room a few metres ahead. The bulb outside of the room was flickering on and off, as if being continually triggered by movement, but I was the only one in the corridor.

My body instinctively tensed.

I began to walk slowly towards the room, my hands balled into fists. When I got close enough I could see something swinging gently through the gap at the hinge. It must have been what was triggering the light.

I inched further forward and leaned sideways to peer around the door. The first thing I saw was a large pair of bare feet floating at face height, bluish toes pointed down towards the floor.

My gaze travelled upwards to a pair of grey trousers and a naked, flabby torso. I knew who it was before I got to the face.

Logue.

One end of a belt had been fastened around his neck and the other had been tied to a light fixture on the ceiling. His wide, open eyes were wet-looking and bulging out of his head, and a purple, bloodied tongue was hanging from his mouth. The ceiling creaked gently like a rocking chair as his body swung from side to side.

It took a few seconds before it dawned on me that he was dead. I had never seen a body look like that before.

A million thoughts erupted in my brain. He had done this to himself. *To himself.* Security would need to be called. Forensics. Don't touch anything. He would need an autopsy – no, *it* would require an autopsy. Logue wasn't alive anymore, he wasn't here. Logue was dead. I would never speak to him again. What would happen to his cottage? Who would have his belongings?

A hot, chunky liquid spurted up into my mouth and I turned away to release the vomit onto the floor.

Had it been painful? How long does it take to die from hanging? As I looked back at his bloated body I fought the urge to pull at the ankles and tear it down. Death shouldn't have such an impact. It shouldn't be on display like this. Logue had managed to wreck so much of what was important to me in the briefest amount of time.

I couldn't look at him anymore.

It, I couldn't look at *it*.

I turned around to face my small splatter of vomit, wondering whether to clean it up. Was it evidence?

# 25

He was staring intently at the smooth wood grain finish on the desk, his long, thin nose casting a shadow over his upper lip. With such unrelenting focus I could see why so many were intimidated by him – even the press had been reluctant to question him too thoroughly – but Watts was a simple man. His ambitions were shallow, immediate and short-sighted. All he wanted was ticked boxes. He was clearly struggling to give a genuine fuck about Logue and what he had done, not because he was cold-hearted but because it was such a meaningless event. Why waste time over something that had ended as soon as it had begun? He was frustrated and wanted to move on from the situation, but he was being forced to dwell on it.

"An investigation is pending," he had said in the speeches made to the press, public, staff and patients, "and we are devastated by the loss of William Logue. That being said, we cannot and will not allow this tragic event to have an impact on the welfare of our patients. We must continue to help those who ask for it."

"But why did he do it?" was the question on everyone's lips. "Why didn't *he* ask for relief?"

To that, Watts' response was always the same. "An investigation is pending."

It had been far worse for me, I'm sure he would have agreed. The security guards had handcuffed me immediately upon arriving at the scene, and shoved me into an empty room, their panicked yells merging into an obscene frenzy that woke up half the facility. I heard one of them shouting into her handheld for the police, claiming a psychotic euthanasist had fought and murdered a colleague in cold blood. It was only then that I considered how incriminating my injuries appeared.

The police came two hours later. They cleared the entire floor except for me, the body and the first few security guards on the scene. After forensics had completed a few tests they concluded that I had nothing to do with Logue's death, but the police proceeded to question me.

I spoke for five hours without food, water or toilet breaks, repeating over and over why I was there, why I had injuries to my face and body, and why I thought Logue had killed himself. Each officer listened politely, told me they understood why I hadn't pressed charges against Mr Myre and agreed that I couldn't have had anything to do with Logue's situation. Yet they didn't stop.

Just as the dizziness began to overwhelm me and the pain in my bladder grew so acute that I had settled on the idea of urinating myself, Watts forced his way into the room. I can't quite remember what he said, but the police soon allowed me to visit the bathroom. Watts then took me straight to his office where a squashed sandwich, biscuits, a couple of pieces of fruit and a glass of water were waiting for me. I drank first, enjoying the sting of the cold water as it slid down my hoarse throat.

Watts did nothing but watch me chew for a while, so I knew he was desperate to say something. I put down the sandwich as if finished, but in reality the stale bread had awoken a raging hunger in me that I had to suppress by kneading my growling stomach with my knuckles.

"How are you feeling?" he asked.

"Fine."

"Are you sure you're okay? I can't believe how long the police kept you. They went way too far. I should file a complaint or…"

"Did you want to talk to me about something?"

He gave me a look of genuine gratitude. "Yes, actually. I need you to take your VDA case to committee tomorrow."

As soon as those words were spoken I became uncomfortably alert. The energy coursing through my body built up so fast it was almost painful.

"While you were with the police I had a quick review of the case notes," he said, choosing to ignore my mounting distress, "and it seems like everything's in place. I requested for the patient to be put to committee tomorrow afternoon. I'll be well into the official investigation on Logue by then so I can't assist in any way, but I think you'll be fine."

"No." It was the only thing my brain could come up with to end Watts' tirade against my work.

Watts sighed. "We don't have time for this. I know you've really thrown yourself into the case and you obviously want to take your time with it, but there'll be other patients and opportunities for that."

"You can't do this."

"It's too late in the day. The committee are preparing for the case as we speak, so that's that. It's done."

"Have you even read my notes?"

"I just told you I have, Nieve, and I must say the level of detail you've used is quite unnecessary. And before you ask, yes, I have seen the archived clips from his diary, and it's more than enough to get the case approved. I mean, for Christ's sake, he starved himself for years, self-harmed, cut himself off from everyone he knew, removed every molecule of himself from his apartment – he's as good as gone as far as he's concerned. He's as good as gone as far as I'm concerned."

"But Valerie and…"

"The parents and Trent and the doctors? Yes, I've heard all of that before. I've also heard you altered his diet plan to lower his nutritional intake. Was that to give yourself more time to prove your desistance theory?"

The warmth drained from me.

"I've read all about that as well. Personal files aren't private." His gaze flickered briefly to the right to ensure the office door was closed. "I have access to everything, even your never-ending journal entries. Don't look so shocked, surely you knew what I had access to, being as smart as you are? And for what it's worth I think you're onto something with this desistance thing, it's promising. I'm more than happy to fund any research you need and provide assistants and equipment – but in about six months or so when everything's blown over. For now we need to save this facility from falling on its arse."

I felt humiliated. Knowing he had seen all of my immature ideas, my notes, my questions…all of it, it was just too much. And there was no remorse in him, no admittance of any wrongdoing. I hated him.

Watts nodded as if hearing my thoughts. "I know you feel like I've betrayed you, but I'm doing the exact opposite. I'm saving you. I'm saving your career. You know, I can see the whole facility running under your command once I'm gone. You're the future of relief, Nieve, I know it. You have the drive and the skill to get anywhere, and I promise you'll be able to start proving that once you've helped us get out this mess."

"We can't just race him through the system. There's a protocol. Without the protocol, we don't have anything."

"No, without the facility we don't have anything."

"You're asking me to ignore evidence just so the reputation of Boar House remains intact. Do you hear yourself? We're not gods, there has to be rules when it comes to relieving patients of their life."

Watts groaned. "If you want the perfect outcome to the perfect situation you're in the wrong field. Look, say you had two identical twins and they lived identical lives, would they would die naturally at the exact same time?"

I shrugged.

"Of course not. That's because death is random, strange and unfair. There are no set rules in nature. What we're doing here is beyond god-like, don't you see? God is cruel because there's no fate or reward or punishment in the natural world, just accidental suffering for some and not for others. Your VDA patient admitted himself for relief because he wants control over his own existence. Yes, what I'm doing is technically against protocol, but ultimately everything points in the same direction. It's still a positive change. Would you rather fail him now and as a consequence ruin his life, his death, your career, my career and the lives of hundreds and thousands of patients when the facility is closed down? Do you want those brainless protesters to win? Do you want to force people to die like Logue did?"

I imagined the thick purple tongue hanging out of grey lips, the bulging, wet eyes… I gagged and just about managed to get to Watts' ornamental wastepaper basket in time. He passed me a bottle of water, but even after I had downed it I could still taste the hot bile in my throat.

Watts grimaced as he picked up the basket and placed it outside the office door. "It's just out there," he said, holding out a handkerchief for me. I pressed it against my lips, feeling the nausea slowly ebb away with the image of Logue.

"Why did he do it?" I asked, not particularly to Watts but rather to get the question out of my head.

"Maybe he was ashamed."

"Of what?"

"Of wanting relief."

"Why? Why would he be ashamed of the one thing he fought for his entire life? It's the only good thing he's ever done. It's the only thing he'll ever be known for."

He sat back down and smoothed out his tie. "There was a big movement years ago where people died by their own hand rather than coming to facilities. Some claimed it was more dignified that way, more natural, but I don't know. Maybe Logue was thinking along those lines."

"Why would anyone turn their death into a statement?" I swallowed hard, determined not to vomit again.

He shrugged, his leg beginning to bounce up and down underneath his desk. He was done and wanted me out of his office.

"Look, take the rest of the day off so you can wake up fresh for the committee tomorrow," he said, standing up to hold the door open while trying to avoid looking at the basket outside. "Once the investigation for Logue is over we'll have a talk about your future with Boar House. We'll do all of this properly, I promise."

I shakily stepped out, the bones in my legs feeling gelatinous.

"Don't forget, Nieve," he said, his eyes gently piercing me like a knife slowly entering flesh, "we've got to stick together in times like these. I've got your back. I hope you have mine."

I inhaled deeply. "Yes, sir," I said. I didn't know what else to say. I was too tired to think.

"Oh, and one more thing." Watts trotted back to his desk and rummaged through one of the drawers. He came back with a small plastic case that he placed in my hand. When I opened it there was a mound of thick, beige cream inside.

"What's this?"

"Makeup. They use it downstairs to cover blemishes. Don't worry, this one is brand new and hasn't been used on anything, I just thought you should put it on before seeing the committee tomorrow. Your skin looks sore and they're bound to ask questions about it. Is that okay?"

"Yes, sir." I nodded as I put the case in my pocket.

When I closed the door behind me I caught the eye of a cleaner putting the vomited-soaked basket into a plastic bag. She smiled pleasantly, as if she were more than happy to clean up my half-melted, chewed up sandwich crusts.

# 26

The committee members arrived in single file, each acknowledging my presence with a weak smile and a nod. Once they were all sat down behind the long, white tablet they clicked buttons on their handhelds, fidgeted and generally ignored one another until the arrival of Professor Riley Smalls, the most senior member of the committee. I had skimmed through a few of his textbooks on patient experience a few years before I began my training. They were fairly informative yet dull.

"Good afternoon everyone," Professor Smalls said, making his way to his seat in the middle of the table. "For the sake of the record, we are joined today for the Voluntary Domestic Aid hearing of Mr David Jonathan Myre with Boar House euthanasist, Nieve Hindeman." Professor Smalls' voice was flat and careful as he held the e-Noter closer than was necessary to his downturned mouth.

The other members of the panel were introduced to me one by one. On the far left was Jade Punter, a sharp-looking woman with a shaved head, followed by the infamous Giorna Przyberow, a man unknown to me named Kyle Smitt, the up-and-coming Lorna Pascal and the perpetual yes-man Charles Buckers.

The moment Professor Smalls began going through the legal information I became aware of a detachment from myself. I wasn't sure if it had only just started or whether I had only just acknowledged it, but I felt weightless yet immoveable. I was static air. There was some sort of barrier between my thoughts and the receipt of my thoughts. I was in a bubble. I looked to my hands. I lifted them up and I moved them, I felt them and controlled them yet I had no idea what they were or why they were rotating in such a way. They looked thicker and heavier but tiny and far away all at once. My heart began to beat faster and I knew there were goosebumps spreading across the entirety of my arms and legs, but I couldn't register the fear. My lungs began to hurt and my lips parted to take in more air, but I felt nothing. I was in a numb state of panic.

"Nieve?"

I looked up and nodded, but those movements were all involuntary. I was nothing but a spectator.

"Would you like to present your case?"

I – or rather, my body – stood and moved towards the back wall where the projector had been set up. The first slide was already up and showing David's face, his name and a short overview of his application.

The detachment made it easier to talk about David. His video diaries, weight loss and self-harm were now random phrases that I was simply relaying to the committee, rather than connected pieces of evidence that meant anything. I described his isolation, his lack of self-worth and the fact that he was disowned by his parents without once thinking about the meaning of the words that left my mouth. An assortment of clips and photographs were shown, and as the last slide compared the downward trend of test results to the upward trend of his physical health, I was starting to enjoy the sensation of merely drifting along.

“Thank you,” Professor Smalls said.

I must have stopped talking.

I sat back down, mildly surprised that the chair managed to hold me. I had assumed the momentum of my body was going to make me sink straight through it, through the floor and further and further downwards, but I was still.

Smalls didn’t seem to notice my thoughts, even though the noise they were making was drowning out my own voice. “The committee members will now have the opportunity to ask some questions,” he said. “I must stress to my colleagues that this is the only chance to query the case with Miss Hindeman before a decision must be made, so please ask anything and everything that comes to mind.”

The questions were rolled very casually in my direction. I had programmed responses for all of them, even when asked why David’s weight stopped increasing near the end of the case. “A miscommunication amongst phys aids,” I said. They moved on without hesitation.

As predicted, their concerns centred on Logue. Had he much of an input on the patient’s treatment? Had his death affected the patient’s mental stability? Had Logue’s involvement with the patient inspired him to do what he did?

“There was very little interaction between them,” I said, sensing my mouth stiffen into a reassuring smile. “As you know, during the first four weeks the patient received nothing but basic care. I believe Logue only met David once during that time. Not long after that I was introduced to the case and had complete control of all treatment. I don’t believe Logue saw the patient alone at all after that.

I'm quite confident Logue did not detrimentally affect the patient, nor did the patient detrimentally affect Logue."

The committee all nodded and typed notes to themselves. One of them muttered something and they all hmmed and ohhed.

"I have a question," Lorna Pascal said, raising her hand. The others looked at her with mild contempt, but I couldn't quite figure out why. "I just wanted to ask about this…Valerie Harmon person. There's a lot of information about her on the file but not so much about her parents or brother. I'm just a little curious about that as David visited the family home a lot."

"It wasn't necessary to speak with them," I said. "Valerie was the only one he spoke to and the house was empty when he visited."

"Can you be sure of that?"

"Yes, I can be," I said, feeling a spark of annoyance somewhere within my deadened body.

"You visited David's old apartment, why not visit the Harmon household as well? Since he spent so much time there?"

"A new family live at that residence now. There would have been no reason to go there."

Pascal nodded but continued to frown. "Do you think further investigation may be required?"

The rest of the committee began whispering, but Pascal continued to stare straight at me. I felt a semblance of life, of deep warmth, travel from my feet and spread up to my legs.

"I don't think that's an appropriate question to ask," Professor Smalls said, shooting a warning look at Pascal. "Don't answer that, Miss Hindeman."

“I...” The mechanics governing my speech couldn’t process the question quickly enough, and the warmth died away. A blanket of silence descended on the room as I lowered my gaze to the table.

Smalls cleared his throat. “Well, I think we should leave things there.” He stood and indicated for everyone else to do the same. “We’ll be in touch within seventy-two hours.”

And that was that.

They all filed out in a row, one by one, giving me the same nod and smile they had entered with. They were one giant entity, a snake with several heads, and the moment they slithered out a tingling sensation spread through my body.

It dawned on me what had just happened. It was all over.

# 27

Had I killed Logue?

It was a strange concept, to think my words had pushed Logue to kill himself. I hadn't believed that kind of power could exist within me. Coactucin was the closest I had ever come to controlling the fate of another person, but I had only ever moved that power from the committee to the intended patient. I had never been personally responsible for a death before, and it felt heavy and cumbersome on me. Like wet clothes.

The idea of feeling that again with David was inconceivable. I didn't want to be the sole commander of another man's existence. It made things too complicated. How could I provide relief for other patients knowing what I was capable of? How could I trust my own judgement?

I had no choice but to return to the Hub to work on David's case. Even if the committee rejected my findings I had to know what I was responsible for.

And it's not like I was busy doing anything else. I should have been preparing for my next patient while the committee made their decision, but I was without one for the first time in my career. I'd heard nothing from Watts about my workload after David; if I didn't prove myself to him soon I would become the next Logue, hidden in plain sight and kept on the payroll out of political embarrassment. Patients would be kept from me, confidential information would bypass me and I would be roaming the halls like a restless ghost.

I was too young for my career to die like that.

I set up camp in a corner of the Hub with David's memory cards scattered around me. Having seen just over half of them already I knew I had to steel myself for hours of scripted repetition. David's three main subjects were his lack of motivation, his boredom and his desire to die; his imagination was seemingly unable to stretch to anything else.

After just one hour I began to lose my patience. David had started to introduce each entry by saying, "Back again," a new infuriating catchphrase that only served to highlight his enjoyment of reiterating past entries word-for-word. Those two words quickly had a Pavlovian effect for me, triggering instantaneous annoyance that worsened every time I heard them.

The self-harm soon became just as frustrating as his soliloquies, their regularity just another dull staple to be included in the diaries. David would reveal fresh wounds on his arms and legs every seven or eight entries, each time with an even number of thin, precise slices on his skin.

"Did this today," he'd say, holding up his still-bleeding forearm like a prize he didn't want. "It just got too much again. It was the only way I could get through the day."

His insincerity was beyond insulting. He wasn't even trying by that point.

By the ninth hour I had hurled a chair across the room, which caused a psych aid to scurry from the Hub like an uncovered beetle. Unsatisfied, I picked up another chair, and another and another and another, furious that my meagre strength had failed to make so much as a dent on a wall or a crack on a window. I sagged to the floor, feeling the warm, fresh blood seeping through my bandages.

Eventually, I crawled back to the work station, nails pressed into my palms and teeth clamped onto my tongue, and I forced myself to watch as David's weight dropped, his skin grew coarser and the shadows under his eyes darkened. Even as he deteriorated he faked every emotion, expression and movement, even when he began to look really ill he was still lying about the same things, playing with me, playing with the audience. I bit the inside of my cheeks, punched my legs, scratched at my arms, did everything to keep myself focused and rooted to that spot in front of the screen.

I needed that pain.

We mistake pain for an error, a side effect, something to be smothered and taken away, but it's a solution to a problem rather than a symptom of it. When a person with paralysis is hurt, the brain can't pick up on the body's signals to deal with the issue, so their heart rate and blood pressure skyrockets in response to the body's cries for help. Something as minor as a foot squashed into a too-small shoe can send a quadriplegic body into overdrive and kill it if the situation is not addressed quickly enough. The patient wouldn't feel a thing, but they'd soon stop existing.

If there is no pain there is no change, and without change the only thing left is death.

And it was that need for pain, that need for change, which ultimately led me to my discovery. After sixteen and a half hours of watching the diaries, if I hadn't given myself a quick, sharp slap across the face to wake myself up, I would have fallen asleep and missed the entry that had begun with David sitting down.

That had never happened before. The footage always started with him switching on the camera off-screen before fumbling back to his chair, but there he was – seated with his arms wrapped round himself, looking lost and frightened. He was quivering. I had forgotten he had once been that thin, with skin so delicate it could barely contain his bones.

"What?"

There was a voice behind the camera. A male voice. Someone was with him, watching him like I was. I leant forward and cupped the headphones with my hands, determined to hear every word.

"Start, David. Come on. Just start, will you?"

David sighed and blinked slowly at the person behind the camera.

"What do you want?" the voice asked. "Just start talking."

David jolted and inhaled deeply, as if suddenly remembering to breathe. "Back again," he said, his voice thick. "Back again. Back again. Back again."

"Come on, David, will you just…"

"Love is between two people, right?"

"*David.*"

"Love is between two people, not one. That's what you said. Love isn't real if only one person can feel it. That's what you told me, right?"

"I'm going to have to edit all this out."

"It wasn't real, was it?"

There was a brief pause, and then, "No."

Tears welled in David's eyes. "No. It wasn't real. So how long now? How long do I have to be here? How long do I have to keep doing this?"

"Logue said another three months to be safe."

I jumped toward the screen, knocking memory cards onto the floor.

"Okay, three months," David said. He mulled over his own words, mouthing them silently to himself. He nodded. "Right, so back again. Back again. Let's go through my day, shall we?"

And then he reverted back to the David he had been in all the other entries. The words, the intonation, the expression, like a switch the emotion left him and something else took over. He blinked rapidly until his eyes stopped gleaming with tears, then started to say the same old nonsense again.

I skipped to the next entry.

"Back again."

And the next.

"Back again."

And the next and the next and the next.

"Back again."

I got on my hands and knees, scrabbling through the cards with fingers shaking so violently I could barely grip anything. Eventually I found it, the last card, labelled one hundred and forty-four, and after several attempts I managed to push the damn thing into the machine.

"Back again."

His skeletal body was sliding down the chair as he spoke, and his voice had changed somehow – the pitch was higher, and he was definitely speaking much slower with a slight slur.

I watched for forty minutes. It was the same as every other entry; only in this one he couldn't disguise his pain.

But it didn't matter, because it was already there. I had already seen it. David had somehow known Logue before Boar House, and someone was with him in that room and helping him to record. He was trained. Coached. He was put through the system. He shouldn't have been there, that much had been proven now.

But why? Why would he fake his way through the system? What was the point?

I had to see him, but the adrenaline was still governing my body and making it almost impossible to pick the cards up from the floor. I stood up with the bag and, swaying slightly, walked out of the room feeling as though I was stepping on a bed of springs.

It was like time had skipped and I was suddenly there, standing outside of David's room. I was looking in on a healthy man with a neat haircut – completely different to the person I had just spent hours watching. He was lying on the bed staring at the ceiling, his mind on either something or nothing, it was hard to tell. I wanted to peel back his scalp and look inside, see if anything was actually moving or whether it was all just pretence.

*Why*. Why did Logue help him? Why did anyone help him?

I had to type in the code four times before I finally got myself inside. David sat up as I approached, wide-eyed and saturated in his own lies. How had I not smelt that on him before?

"You knew him," I said. I wanted to get the words out before I had the chance to mull them over.

He raised his eyebrows in an attempt to convey surprise. The expression was neither too subtle nor overtly exaggerated, but it was still so rehearsed it made me squirm to look at him. Would I have found that at all convincing before?

"Who did I know?" he asked.

"Logue. You knew him."

"Logue? You mean the doctor who killed himself?"

I faltered – I didn't think anyone would have told him about that. Surely the psych aids would have felt that telling him would compromise his treatment? Unless he knew more people in the facility. I tried to think who it could have been.

"He was a euthanasist, not doctor. And don't bullshit me. You knew Logue before you came here."

"I don't…"

"I watched your videos."

He nodded slowly. "I made a video journal, yes, but I honestly don't know what you're talking about."

"You *knew* him."

"What makes you say that?"

I took out my e-Noter and played the clip to him. His arrogance crumbled into a wince as he listened to the pitiful whines he had made to the man behind the camera. By the end he couldn't even look at the screen.

"Who was in the room with you?" I asked.

"Does it matter?"

"Yes."

"Why?"

"I need to know."

"You really don't, you don't need to know anything," he said, looking to one of the cameras.

"They're not on, I switched them off before I got here. Do you really think I want anyone finding out about this yet?"

"Prove it."

I went to the nearest camera, took off my shoe and repeatedly slammed the heel into the side of it until the bracket broke from the wall. When I came back David was cowering slightly, eyeing the shoe in my hand.

"Jesus, you're insane."

"Well? Who was it? You might as well tell me."

He swallowed. "Trent."

"I knew it."

He snorted. "Then why ask?"

I suddenly felt very weak. My knees buckled and I fell to the floor, only just managing to hold my hands out in time to stop my face from slamming into the ground. I pressed my cold hands to my face to try and block out the pain that was squeezing my head so tightly, but it only made me focus on it more.

I was fucked. This was going to be on me, all of it, I wasn't sure how but Watts would make sure of it. I'd be thrown out. No, worse, I'd be forced to stay and keep quiet. He'd do everything in his power to ensure it was kept in-house. And what then? I'd just be trapped for the rest of my life, always knowing that if I made the slightest mistake I'd be out or arrested on some irrelevant charge – he'd come up with something like fraud or theft, nothing to do with the patients or my work. Nothing too scandalous. Maybe there would even be a terminal diagnosis and I'd be offered relief.

"You need to tell me everything," I said.

David was peering down at me from the bed, a look of genuine concern on his face. I hated that.

He didn't respond at first, just sank back into himself, so I got up and locked the door with the overriding code and covered the two-way glass with a spare blanket.

"What are you doing?" he asked, swinging his legs over the side of the bed as if preparing to jump and run, but there was nowhere for him to go. There was nowhere for either of us to go.

"Tell me everything," I said again.

He laughed in a spiteful, mocking way, but his hands were gripping the mattress so tightly his knuckles had turned white. "Do you honestly think I'm going to do anything you tell me to do? I'm here to die, remember? I've been starved, cut, isolated, bored out of my fucking brain…do you really think you can make me do anything I don't want to do?"

"Why are you here?"

"I've told you a thousand times. I'm here to die, nothing else. That's the only goal here, the only thing I came here to do. Everything else is irrelevant."

"But why?"

He laughed again, but the malice had already faded. "Christ, it wasn't my idea. Death is never anyone's first choice."

"Whose idea was it?"

Silence.

"Look," I said, "this is about me now. Logue's dead, I'm sure Trent can take care of himself and the committee's got complete control of your case, so I can't stop you from getting what you want. This is just about my career – my *life* – and it's all on the line because of you.

You've put me in it, and I need to know what's going on so I can get myself out of it. I don't care if you live or die. I really don't. It's gone way past that. Maybe I'll have to learn to live with that some day, but right now you need to help me figure out a way of getting through the next few days."

"But you don't know anything, so you're fine. You're innocent."

"Ignorance isn't innocence. If I can't see what's coming I can't get out of the way."

"But I *have* to die."

"I told you, that's not up to me. That's up to the committee."

"So you won't try and stop it?"

"I can't. I wouldn't."

His long, slender fingers reached up to tug at his hair, a nervous twitch to accompany his thoughts, but when he realised the hair was too short he pinched the skin at the back of his neck instead. He then began tapping his foot, slowly at first, but then the movements became so fast and so forceful it was as if jolts of electricity were jumping through his leg.

"My mum and dad," he suddenly blurted out. "It was them. They wanted me to come here."

"That's not hard to believe. But why?"

"It was better than the alternative."

"Which was?"

His leg tapping slowed, and his head began to nod at the same rhythmic pace. "Shame for them. Prison for me."

"Prison? What did you do?"

"I fell in love with someone I shouldn't have."

"Valerie."

"No."

"Then who?"

He swallowed. "Dan."

"Dan?" It took me a few seconds to realise who he was talking about. "Her brother? But he's…"

"He was. He's eighteen now."

"But he wasn't six years ago, was he?"

A cold sickness spilled into my gut. What a waste. What a stupid, pointless waste of so many lives. Of all my time. "That's why you went to their house…"

"It began before then. By the time I stopped going to work he'd become everything." He watched me, clearly waiting for me to say something to show my disgust, but I wouldn't. "I told Valerie I'd got a new job working from home but my apartment was too much of a distraction, so she offered me her keys. She was a good friend, really. She had no idea that Dan was staying home from school with me. He's really smart, you know. He managed to hack into his school records so it looked like he was going in every day, and he passed all his exams because he could teach himself anything. Honestly, he's really *that* clever. He read about three books a week, and not just fiction, he'd read all about history and science. He actually taught himself. Can you imagine that? Someone being their own teacher? He taught me stuff all the time, and…"

"*Shut up*."

His excitement immediately dissolved and I took great pleasure in watching the shame seep back in.

"Do his parents know?"

"No."

"But Valerie does."

"Yes. She…"

"I don't want to know how she found out. So why didn't she call the police?"

"She almost did, but Dan persuaded her not to. He said it'd break their parents apart and it'd ruin his life if the school found out he'd not been in for months. She agreed, but only if I stayed away. I didn't, so she told my mum and dad about us. Dad beat the shit out of me. Mum cried. But they didn't want to go to the police either because they'd heard about a couple who…when the police found out that one of their kids was…" He paused. "Their lives would be ruined if they said anything.

"But Dad felt he had to do something about it, and then he remembered a guy he used to know at university. That was Logue. Logue got us in touch with Trent, who's helped with this kind of thing before, and Trent said I had to go into hiding for a few years to make sure none of this could be traced back. That's why he made me make those fucking video diaries and promise never to leave the apartment.

"Mum and Dad had to give money to Trent, Logue and Valerie, as well as pay for my rent and buy me food while I was shut in. I've ruined my parents financially, I've broken them, I've ruined everything. This is how I'm going to pay them back."

"And that boy? Dan? How are you going to pay him back for what you've done to him? What you've taken from him?"

He shook his head. "But I don't feel like I've taken anything, I've given him everything. I'm giving him my life."

"You're proud of this?"

"I would do it all over again if I could. I suppose that's why this needs to happen, because people who are truly evil never think they are."

"So you want to die?"

"No. I need to die."

"But what am I supposed to do?"

"You? Nothing. It's all done."

"But you've ruined me too. All for nothing. Logue…he killed himself because I almost found out. All this is on *me*."

"Why? You didn't do anything and no one else has to know. You even said it's all in the committee's hands now, and when I'm gone you don't have to worry about any of this anymore."

"Do you honestly think they won't pin this on me if it gets out? They'll need someone to blame. And it's not just that, god knows how many people have been murdered over the years because of Trent. Maybe he'll carry on doing it. Maybe he'll find another euthanasist to help him. Or maybe it's bigger than him? Maybe he's just a small cog in the machine? How far does this go?"

"He's just been getting rid of people like me, people who've fallen through the cracks and aren't able get relief the normal way. He's doing the right thing."

"Logue killed himself. Is that the action of a man who's done the right thing?"

"He was doing the right thing for the wrong reasons."

"But everyone does that, that's human nature. Altruism doesn't exist. I help people find relief because I'm good at it, because it makes me feel like I'm doing something worthwhile, not because I want to kill people. What kind of person would that make me? That's psychopathic."

"What's your point?"

"My point is, if Logue was doing the right thing he would have been able to live with it."

David shrugged.

My chest hurt, and I realised I'd been holding my breath for some time. "I can't do this," I said, exhaling slowly.

"What choice do you have?"

What choice *did* I have?

I could have killed David there and then to stop him from muddying the profession further. A sort of sacrifice, if you will, to cut out the rot. I could have pretended to uncover the truth after the fact, but god knows how I could have done that convincingly. I could have found Trent and forced him to confess, but something told me that would have been an impossible feat – on both parts. I could have tried to prove desistance and David's lack thereof to prove he wasn't viable for relief, but Watts would have simply removed me from the facility before the information could have made much of an impact.

I could have done a lot of things, but whatever I chose to do David would have ended up in the same state and I would have been in a worse one.

"You're right," I said, my panic disappearing so quickly it was almost like it was never there. "I have no choice."

# 28

They took forty-eight hours to reach a decision. Just forty-eight hours to decide whether a patient they had never met lived or died. At least half of that time must have been spent sleeping, eating, drinking and toileting, and their thoughts must have drifted from the case every now and then, so how much time did that leave? Twenty hours? Maybe less? I hadn't really considered the committee's process like that before – did not knowing make the decision quicker? Easier? Fairer? Juries never meet the accused before the trial, but does that make them unbiased, or just unprepared? Who decided to make impartiality such an important factor in these sorts of things?

Like a morbid procession, they came in one-by-one – Smalls, Punter, Przyberow, Buckers, but no Pascal. There was an enforced solemnity that hadn't been there the last time. There was no greeting, nod or eye contact from any of them. This was their ritual, their parade of death.

Everyone sat down except for Smalls, who addressed the empty room as though it were filled with an eagerly anticipated audience.

"Good morning, everyone," he said. His voice was more animated than usual, probably because this would be the only statement of his that students would listen to if they studied the case. "I, Professor Riley Smalls, am speaking on behalf of the Humanitarian Governing

Committee to present euthanasist, Nieve Hindeman, with the relief verdict for Voluntary Domestic Aid patient, David Myre.

"Unfortunately Lorna Pascal from the HGC will not be joining us today due to illness. I have a compliance document from her that I shall now present to Miss Hindeman."

A notification appeared on my e-Noter. The document was short and simply stated that Pascal had agreed with the verdict as decided by the committee. Her digital signature ran along the bottom of the screen.

"Nieve Hindeman, please confirm receipt and acceptance of Lorna Pascal's compliance document."

I nodded. "Yes, received and accepted."

Smalls gave an audible sigh of relief. Watts must have warned him about me. Then again, if the circumstances had been different I would have called for the verdict to be rescheduled so that Pascal could attend – it was, after all, my right as euthanasist to have the entire committee present.

And then the formalities began; there were numerous verbal and written agreements, reminders of particular laws as well as an overview of the entire case to sit through. It was obvious – at least to me – that this section of the verdict was purposefully drawn out to break the tension in the room. Boredom also makes people eager to comply.

Before the Myre case I listened closely to every word and drank in every detail. I was eager for the opportunity to highlight a misread word or an overlooked error, but David stripped me of that excitement. None of it was real. It was all a ruse, and the committee were oblivious it.

Or were they? If Logue was involved, what's to say Watts wasn't? And Smalls? And members of the government? It may seem as though paranoia was beginning to drown out every logical thought in my head, but how did David get through the system so smoothly if more people weren't involved? Incompetency and luck can only get you so far. And those kinds of things can't be manufactured so effortlessly, not when a life is at stake.

Someone at that table must have known. David said it was going to die with him, but the rot went far deeper. He wasn't the carcass, he was merely a fly sitting on top of it. I looked into each of the committee member's eyes for a few seconds, looking for signs of wrongdoing, but they just stared dumbly back like cattle.

Smalls suddenly fell quiet and looked at me expectantly.

"Miss Hindeman?"

"Sorry, Professor, I…"

"I asked whether you're ready for the verdict."

What a question. It was a question that only warranted one answer, making it the most difficult sentence I've ever had to respond to.

The words sat in the forefront of my mind, but when I eventually said, "Please proceed, Professor," they didn't sound right out loud.

Smalls looked to the others and they nodded sagely, all swelling with importance.

As he rested his hands on his stomach ready to deliver his final speech, I noticed his smooth, bald head was not the least bit shiny. The skin was clean and dry and powdered ready for the occasion – as was his face, which had an unnaturally smooth finish to it. I then realised the other committee members had also made considerable effort with their appearance and were wearing smart, brand new clothes accentuated with jewellery and accessories. This was an important outing for them – but not for David, of course. He had no idea what was happening at that moment and would never get to recognise the faces of those who had such a hold over his fate, no matter what the outcome turned out to be. It's unfair that the identity of the committee is hidden from the public yet has complete access to their lives.

In unison, as if they had all heard a sound my ears couldn't detect, the committee members shifted in their seats and looked up at Smalls. He responded by clearing his throat to ensure no phlegm or saliva would obstruct his moment.

"No two VDA cases are ever the same," he began, putting unnecessary emphasis on each word, "but some don't quite unfold as expected. This was one such case for us. What initially seemed to be the straightforward plight of a man with nothing to live for, who displayed self-harm, body dysmorphia and self-incurred isolation, became a complex and problematic case marred by a myriad of issues – some preventable, but most unavoidable in nature.

"I think it's been noted by all that David has been consistently eager for his wishes to be met. The committee have viewed this impatience in both a positive and negative light as, although he has been vocal in communicating exactly what he wants, his desperation could be seen as a mere by-product of his personality type. How can you tell the difference between what a man needs and what a man wants, or has decided that he wants? Or is there even a distinction? Should there be a distinction with these matters? This is a question we ask ourselves with every case, but it has been a dominating topic with David.

"The committee spent a lot of time discussing what would happen to David if he wasn't given relief. We can't see a future for him after this, and David definitely hasn't considered his existence as an option, but is that reason enough? Just because he has nothing to live for right now, does that mean he shouldn't have a future? Again, this is a common VDA question that this case has called particular attention to, and I would like to be able to answer this before my career is over. I would like a clear, definitive answer, but will I ever get one? Is this possible?"

The scream brewing in my throat was difficult to contain. But it wasn't time. David wasn't the one for this.

But if not now, when?

"At the end of the day," Smalls said, interrupting my train of thought, "everything with David has been pushing forward in one particular direction with no apparent deviations, but does that mean we should just approve him? Just because he can't find something to live for now, does that mean he never will? How can we decide if his life is worth living?

"This is a difficult question to answer as it is, but then we have the added complication of how this case was dealt with. In particular, Mr William Logue was a huge concern for us, but with research it seems he was mostly guilty of neglect. He spent very little time with the patient and test results suggest he had no impact on David's progress, but did Logue have a detrimental impact on his colleagues?"

My body stiffened.

"Miss Hindeman, you have been put under a lot of stress for someone of your career level, experience and age. Logue was a hindrance rather than a mentor to you, but although Doctor Watts attempted to steer as much of the responsibility for that onto himself, you have refused his help repeatedly – even to the point of giving yourself more work. This is something I have never seen before and initially didn't know how to interpret.

"The detail put into this case is commendable, but rather than benefitting the outcome I believe it has added confusion to the mix. You have pushed and pushed to get as much information out of this as possible but have seemingly lost sight of what's important. From the committee's perspective we have had too much to work with, and with too much information comes doubt, especially when it comes to instinctual reasoning. You will become a great euthanasist, Miss Hindeman, once you've learned to trust your instincts more and follow your nose, not your research.

"It all comes down to the fact that the committee have been presented with a confident patient and an unconfident euthanasist. It has made us all question our positions in a way we haven't in years, which has been refreshing, but this isn't about us. It's about David. He didn't want to be an experiment or the catalyst of reflection, he wanted results. Has Myre been affected by the length and difficulty of this case? Maybe. Will it affect the outcome? No.

"Therefore, on behalf of the Humanitarian Governing Committee, I am approving David Myre for the relief procedure. He will undergo the procedure in two days, on the twenty-seventh of October, at five-thirty pm. Nieve Hindeman, will you agree to perform this procedure as the patient's euthanasist?"

Someone said, “Yes, sir.” It was probably me.
He nodded, which made the others nod too.
It was done.

# 29

We used the family room to inform VDA patients of the committee's verdict. It was usually the setting for pre-admittance interviews, funeral planning and post-relief reflection, but every now and then it would host a euthanasist and their patient. Both would perch expectantly on the pale blue sofa that stretched across the entirety of the room. Sometimes they would be accompanied by a visitor, but they would always be alone in their discussion.

David was wide-eyed and quiet, his mouth narrow and clamped firmly shut. He looked like he might vomit. I didn't feel much of anything; I was a spectator again and could only watch through muffled unconsciousness. I knew what was happening, knew what was about to happen, but I couldn't do anything about it.

"Are you recording this?" was the first thing he asked. I nodded. "And are people watching us right now?"

"Probably not," I said, but the lie fell flat. "There will be a review of the footage…" I almost added *posthumously*, but luckily my throat stuck before the word emerged.

He looked very fragile. I almost felt sorry for him. I had to keep reminding myself who he was, what he was, in the same way I imagine it must be easy to forget that an elderly person has faults. Or that a child will soon learn to do the most awful things. Weakness encourages weakness.

The words were somewhere deep inside my brain, working their way to the top, but I didn't mind waiting for them. I felt like I had all the time in the world.

"You're killing me here," he said, no hint of irony in his voice.

I wanted a stronger reaction than fear. He didn't deserve to feel that. I wanted to force him to draw the news from me with hostility, with rage. I wanted to laugh and say, "See! I knew all along that was in you." He didn't deserve my pity, but he was getting it anyway. His mouth was twitching, his eyes darting about the place – why was he allowed to be so human-like? He was filth, he was selfishness and destruction, yet I was looking after him, the facility was looking after him, and he was being gently brought out of his existence rather than shoved out kicking and screaming. He should be ripped out of the world and thrown away from it, not tenderly coaxed out.

Did it matter how he went, just so long as he went?

I was sure I knew the answer to that once.

I inhaled until my lungs were so full it felt like I was suffocating. "You've been approved for relief." I hadn't sounded apologetic, thank god, but I had been gentle. Too gentle.

He didn't react much. He just looked off into the distance, his mind comprehending the reality of it all, no doubt. No tears fell from his red-rimmed eyes, but his lips and cheeks did start to tremble. He began to nod, as if agreeing to the decision.

"That's good." I could tell they were filler words with no meaning attached to them. At least he was in shock, I was glad of that. “That’s very good, I’m very pleased to hear that.”

“The procedure will be performed on the twenty-seventh of October. You can spend the next two days however you’d like. You can receive counsel from your psych aid, take walks on the grounds with a phys aid, speak to me…or you can be alone. You can even request the presence of friends or family members if you want, but as you know they’re under no obligation to visit. It would be their choice.”

“I want to be alone.”

“You don’t have to make a decision now.”

“I want to be alone. This is my decision now. *Mine*. No one else’s. I don’t want anyone else to take that away from me, do you understand?”

“Yes.”

“Good. I don’t want counsel. I don’t want people. I want silence. I want to figure out what this really means for me, you know?”

“That’s fine,” I said, although I had no idea what he meant.

He settled back on the sofa. “My life is mine now.”

It wasn’t. It was mine. I’d earned it, not him. I’d fought harder for it than he’d fought for anything. He’d practically given himself away, and for what? For a feeling. For a distraction. Doing that had been the worst crime of his pitiful existence, even if he tried to console himself with the idea that he was evil. He was worse than evil. He was nothing. A waste.

My fury was oblivious to him.

“Do I get a last meal?”

The mechanics took over once again. “We don’t call it that, but you can choose something you’d like to eat twelve hours before the procedure. As you’ll have discussed with your psych aid, you can’t eat anything twelve hours prior to the procedure because…”

“Yes, but I can choose whatever I want before that, right?”

“Yes.”

He grinned with such ferocious warmth that I felt a prickle in my throat. The disappointment was overwhelming.

“I want pasta with cheese.”

“Okay.”

“And prawns. Deep-fried prawns. And orange juice, and potatoes and cream. I’d love a chocolate cake. And pastry. Can I have pastry?”

“Yes.”

He slapped the sofa with excitement. “Then I’m going to have roast chicken too. And the last thing I’m going to have is stuffing, because my mum…” He stopped for a second and thought. He must have realised he’d never see her again. When was the last time he saw her, I wondered? It must have been years.

But then he sighed, and the past seemed to leave him.

In 2012, E.J. Babb sought a platform for which to discuss dystopian fiction – a rather bleak yet, in many ways, hopeful genre – and thus, Dystopic was born.

Dystopic is predominantly dedicated to reviewing and discussing dystopian literature and film, but it also includes sci-fi, horror, speculative fiction, dark comedy and non-fiction.

For more information, visit:
**www.dystopic.co.uk/about-dystopic**

Printed in Great Britain
by Amazon

36687757R00168